SAY I'M YOURS,

Firecracker

TAYLOR WILSON-WEST

Paperback ISBN: 9798988396925

eBook ISBN: 9798988396932

Cover Design by Karley Stafford, Literary Bound Designs

Illustrations by Roze Stojovska

Edited by Trinity McIntosh, Type A Tweaks

Proofread by Tina White & Ashley DePointe

Formatting by Taylor Wilson-West & Trinity McIntosh

To my Grandma Kitty.

Thank you for always believing I would accomplish great things. No matter how wild the dream.

SAY I'M YOURS,
Firecracker

Foreword

Hello my wonderful readers, we meet again. This time for a very different story. One with strong themes. Some of which may make you feel uncomfortable, hopefully you can see the beauty on the other side.

Ronnie and Finn have been the hardest couple to write. They both have a lot going on inside their heads, and neither are good with words. Some things to consider before turning the page.

The loss of family members, attempted suicide (not the main characters), body image, pregnancy loss and infertility are all themes in the book. Although I tried to handle these with gentle care and respect, some content may be upsetting.

If you're interested in reading a story about a woman overcoming her past and learning to love again, and a man wrestling with his value, all while trying to be his best self, this is for you.

I may be biased, but I think these two are worth it.

All my love,

Taylor Wilson-West

Ronnie

Before

"Shots?" I asked as we made our way past Benny with a head nod, into Dusk 'Til Dawn.

"Hell yes!" Xavier hollered over the noise. Bright lights pulsed over the gyrating bodies on the dance floor. Music thrummed through my heels and up my legs. Xavier, one of my best friends, and I decided on having a night out, while Bell, my other best friend, stayed locked up in her house. Sometimes she got in her head a little too far and we both knew it was best to leave her to her own devices.

This was my element, nameless people, strong drinks, and there standing at the railing above the pool of people–stood my mystery man.

He was handsome, and one of the most intriguing men I'd found since moving here a few years ago with Bell. Almost every time I'd come here there he'd be, standing sentry over the black banister. Like some kind of gorgeous gargoyle.

At first, I thought he owned the club. When he was at Dusk 'Til Dawn girls fawned and men clapped his hand, like he was someone everyone knew, and if they didn't, they wanted to.

The bartender, with half her head shaved, swiftly corrected us the last time our little group went dancing. He's the boss's brother, a trust fund kid who had money to blow.

Although, kid isn't the way I'd describe him. No, he exuded an air about him that was definitely not childlike. He oozed sex appeal, and arrogance. The kind of man who knew exactly the kind of reaction he caused.

I imagined under that perfectly styled beard he had a jaw cut from granite. His lips never curved up, instead always staying in a neutral position as if nothing pleased him.

To be frank, he seemed like a pompous dick. Holding court with all the business men, while women clamored over themselves for his attention.

I couldn't help my curiosity, he was beautiful, and I loved beautiful things.

Our eyes locked across the span of the room, I winked and spun around to see the smirk in Xavier's eyes.

"That one doesn't know what he's about to get himself into." He whisper-shouted, mouth turned up, teeth on full display.

"I don't think it's fair of you to assume he's getting anywhere near me at all." I sing-songed back at him.

"Please." He said, eyes cocked to side-eye me. He passed me a shot, we turned them up and drank them down.

When I grabbed Xavier by the hand and pranced onto the dance floor I could feel someone's eyes on me. The heat from his stare had nothing on the press of bodies all around us as we moved.

Xavier made sure to touch me, running his hands along my sides, mussing my wavy hair. He kept his face close to mine as we swayed and dipped.

This week something felt different. I told Xavier in the car on the way over that tonight would be the night I lured him in. Seven solid weekends of flirting with his eyes, if he didn't act tonight I'd assume he was uninterested in taking our playful battle up a notch, and find another willing body to satisfy my cravings.

Xavier found a partner who looked as interested in him as he was in them. As the crowd moved they were swallowed up. I danced, not caring who was touching me as long as they kept it platonic.

I had a goal to accomplish before any below-the-belt play could begin.

Songs changed and the crowd continued to shift until it parted. Like the red fucking sea.

Most of the bodies continued to dance at a slower pace, watching the man from the top floor leisurely walk in my direction. I pretended not to notice him.

Let him believe he's the predator. Instead of my prey.

When I could see the shades of brown in his eyes he stopped, and I had to tilt my head back to really look at him.

I was wrong before.

He wasn't just a pretty boy, fuck, he was stunning. Dark lashes framed dark eyes, his hair was moused and tied back into a half knot behind his head.

Loose waves curled around his shoulders, where tattoos peeked out of his dress shirt.

Good Lord have mercy. He was huge. His shoulders took up enough air space to land a small plane. And his arms, I had to bite my lip to keep from ogling the veins that ran maps down his exposed forearms.

He nodded his head, just slightly, an invitation.

I smiled, looking him up and down as if making a decision. His dark brows rose, as if surprised I didn't jump at his command.

He leaned down, close enough that if I moved his lips would connect with mine. "I could take you right here, but I like to give my lady a bit more privacy." His breath ghosted over my ear and my body erupted in goosebumps.

"Lady, huh?" I laughed, I was no lady.

"Maybe you'd like being fucked in front of strangers." He didn't pose it as a question, but it wasn't a statement either.

I placed a hand on his shoulder, pushing him out of my way. As I walked away from him I made sure to swing my hips, carefully placing my steps so I wouldn't fall on the now slick dance floor.

He caught up quick, his chest licking heat up my spine. His sizable hands clamped down on my waist, "I hope you're okay with me touching you, Firecracker." He rumbled low, and anticipation shot through my veins. "Because I need it."

He steered us into a dark hall, where lights flashed and the wall was velvet.

Tile floor turned to plush carpet before he spun me around and pressed his lips to mine, hungry and unyielding. I'd never been kissed with such determination.

"Every time I've seen you walk through those doors I've wanted to do that." His voice seemed even deeper than before. Honest in a way that surprised me.

"That's a long time to wait, Behemoth."

He trailed his mouth down my neck, over the curve of my jaw. "I don't do this."

"Fuck girls in clubs?"

He laughed, "Fuck girls I don't know."

"No names." I stopped him, planting my lips on his. He got the hint, or at least we both seemed to be on the same page.

His calloused hands roamed over my clothes, pushing or pulling them for better access. I should care that he'd exposed my breasts to anyone who happened to get close enough to our secluded corner. When I chose my sequined silver tank I didn't expect to have it shoved between my breasts like a thong for my tits.

I devoured his sounds, enjoying the wetness pooling beneath my skirt. I'd seen him here often, but always from the dance floor below. His tattooed arms leaned over the railing with a tumbler of dark amber liquid.

Now that I could see him closer I cataloged every inch, memorizing every tattoo to memory. A rose covered one hand, and roman numerals lined his fingers. I was currently too tipsy to understand them.

He wasn't gentle, and neither was I.

Placing his hands on my hips he hoisted me up so we aligned in all the most delicious places. I unbuckled the expensive leather belt from his tailored pants but didn't bother to remove it completely.

I unzipped him and plunged my hand into his boxers. He was girthy, not obnoxiously big, thank God, I never was one to enjoy a nine-inch cock. The way he moved his mouth was ecstasy and I had a feeling he would make me cum, hard. He was shaved, which surprised me. With all the hair on his head and his neatly trimmed beard, I'd thought there would be at least some hair here.

Swiping my thumb across his tip I spread his arousal as he continued his assault on my breasts.

"Fuck." He growled, eyes never leaving mine. He switched to kneading my thigh leaving one hand to roam up my skirt and since we were both impatient, he pushed the material up to my hips exposing me to him.

He pulled a condom out of nowhere, not that I cared enough to ask, and rushed to roll it over his length. I gripped him again, pumping him in my hand before guiding his cock to my entrance, smearing my wetness all over his tip.

Fuck was right, I couldn't wait a minute longer. I pushed off the wall, wrapped one leg around his waist, and arched my back so I could control just how much of him I took.

"Goddam, Firecracker." He hushed out on a breath.

He was barely keeping it together, as I stilled to give him a moment. Leaning into him I said, "Fuck me like you hate me, pretty boy."

His eyes, impossible as it may be, darkened, and he lifted me up wrapping my other leg around his waist and pressing me into the wall. In one fluid movement, he slid all the way to the hilt, crushing my clit into his pelvis. He watched me grind on him like a cat in heat, letting me control the first few movements.

The moment I moaned into his neck, his control snapped, a thin rubber band stretched too thin. He pounded into me, my back hit the wall as his thrusts became harder. He buried himself into me over and over as he watched between my pussy and my face.

His mouth covered mine to stifle our sounds. Flesh hitting flesh, slick sucking, it was all I could hear, even the music seemed muted in this moment.

As waves of pleasure wreaked havoc on my nerves, he continued to press himself as far in as he could, grinding my clit and hitting all the nerves in my body at just the right angle. Heat swept across my skin as my orgasm built closer.

"Cum on my cock, Firecracker." He whispered into my shoulder, before biting down on the sensitive skin there and using the moment to pinch my nipple. Hard.

Cum I did.

I sunk my teeth into his white dress shirt, uncaring of the possible damage. Clamping down I let out a howl of pleasure as he made sure to take every drop of my rapture. Muscles locked, I couldn't hold on anymore from the shaking orgasm he ripped from me.

"Fuck woman." He grunted as he followed me over the cliff. We both stayed there, breaths heavy, muscles sore, and completely spent. Him holding me against the wall, his body blocked most of the traffic back here.

"Let me get you cleaned up." He said, his voice still gravely with sex. He helped me unwind my legs from around his waist, sliding his cock free, and set me back on my feet.

"I can handle a little cum, pretty boy."

"A little?" He said, running his fingers through the mess I'd made on my thighs. The roughness of the calloused pads of his fingers had me shivering. Which wasn't good. I needed to move before this guy could give me his name.

I mourned his dick—because let me be honest, it was a good ride—while I pulled my tank top back across my breasts and pushed my skirt back down around my thighs. He removed the condom and tucked himself away then took a deep breath.

"No. No." I said, placing a finger against his soft puffy lips. "I don't do names."

His eyes went wide, and he parted his lips, but I skirted around him and made for the ladies room.

Safely locked in a stall I cleaned myself up the best I could. Panic set in after the adrenaline wore off. It was a crash of epic proportions.

After all of the teasing and the flirting, I had him. Another pleasurable ride. I had no way to contact him, it's the way I liked it. The way I *needed* it, but now? With his cum dripping out of me, fear planted itself inside of my every pore.

Fuck.

Congratulations

Your baby is the
size of a blueberry.

Ronnie

One

Letting off steam with my best friends was my favorite high. Especially at our local club Dusk 'Til Dawn. We'd been working hard for our current clients. Haven Macemore, country super star, and Adrian Scott, hotel mogul.

It still felt like a fever dream I'd wake up from.

Haven was everything I could have hoped for. She was sweet, and down to earth. I'd loved working with her, especially since I'd been fangirling over her for years.

Her wedding was going to be the best thing we'd ever put together. Bellamy, my best friend and partner at Fixin' To I Do, finally agreed to a girls night out. Even though Xavier, the third to our trio, is a man he's always been a part of our crew.

I was wearing my favorite skimpy dress, with my louboutin heels. I felt powerful and sexy, especially after the last time I was here.

A waitress came by as we were sitting down and I ordered for us. "Rum and coke, lemon drop martini, and I'll have a Jameson." We had a lot to discuss.

Bellamy was in a new relationship, which shocked the hell out of her, but not me. I knew the moment she saw Aaron that they had a connection.

"Now dish, playa!" I said, leaning back in the seat trying not to look up toward the VIP lounge, where I knew *he* would be.

As she told us about her date and how wonderful it went, other than a little hiccup with another woman, our drinks had arrived. Along with the sleazy guy who had been attempting to dance with me all night.

Xavier was usually the best buffer, but seated at this angle all he could do was tell the sleaze to fuck off.

We downed our drinks and set off for the dance floor, music blasted from invisible speakers, lights flashed and sweat rolled down my back as we danced and laughed. My feet started to hurt, and my head was already fuzzy. I couldn't remember the last time a drink had hit me this hard, this fast.

Xavier secured shots and we headed back to our table. Where we could be as loud as we wanted and talked about all the things we hadn't had time to catch up on. I was flying, soaring above the clouds when a hand clamped down on my arm and Bellamy swore.

"Take your hand off her, now." She said, her voice deadly.

I was trying, and failing, to sober up as the sleaze ball attempted to jerk me out of the booth. I yelped as my hip connected to the corner of our table.

The dark club was made even darker when two large shadows fell over our table.

"Unhand the lady." The man with Aaron had a deep rasp that sounded like the reaper himself. "She was just leaving with her friends," he continued. "Weren't you, love?"

My eyes widened, fear tasted sour on my tongue. It was the sexy as fuck guy from the balcony. He was dressed in black slacks, and a white button down, cuffs crisp and dripping wealth.

"No, she and I were about to have some fun." The man's hand clamped harder around my wrist and I might have whimpered. I couldn't tell, I had drunk one drink but my head was already fuzzy. All I knew was he was hurting me, and this big, gorgeous man that I'd fucked in this very club was standing over me, calling me 'love'.

My mystery man threw a meaty hand at the man who had clamped down on my wrist. Blood poured from his nose and over his lips, but his grip didn't loosen.

He pulled me up from the booth, placing my back to his front. I could smell cigarette smoke wafting from his breath as he mumbled something to Aaron's friend.

All hell broke loose. Fists were flying, and then Aaron had the guy with no boundaries in some sort of arm lock that my brain couldn't comprehend.

Then mystery man's hands were on my shoulders, his eyes roaming my body, inch by inch. When he was satisfied he guided me and Xavier toward the door. The air was chilly, and my dress wasn't the warmest thing in my closet.

"I'm sorry." Xavier lifted his hand from where he was standing. "What the hell just happened here?"

"I threw that asshole out a few weeks ago. Same issue," my gargoyle grunted.

"So then, why did he come back?" Bellamy asked, appearing out of nowhere. "What about security? How did he get back in?"

"I'll find out." He was so curt, and almost cold in his response to her. "Until then, I want to know if your friend here is okay."

His chocolate eyes zeroed in on mine. I felt like I couldn't breathe. The man who had haunted my dreams and fantasies ever since we fucked in a secluded corner of this club was starring at me. Speaking to me. Touching me. Concerned about me.

I couldn't stand anymore in these heels. Thoughts swam and my focus started to fade when my mystery man literally swept me off my feet and said, "We'll take my truck."

He held me against his chest like I weighed nothing, and carried me over to a massive truck. Gently, he sat me down in the front seat and all my thoughts went silent as I gave into the exhaustion I'd been fighting all night.

Finn

Two

I followed Aaron to his girl's house, where I guess they had decided they would be staying the night. The guy that was with the girls rode in the back of my cab, he was snoring by the time we pulled up at the curb.

I hopped out, stretching my limbs and rolling up my sleeves. I caught the dirty words Aaron was saying to his girl and chuckled.

The blonde bombshell was softly snoring when I opened the truck door. As easy as I could, I wrapped her in my arms and carried her inside. "Where do you want me to put her?"

The mouthy brunette pointed to the air mattress set up in the tiny living room. I laid her down carefully, and watched as her friend covered her with a blanket.

"Where's Xavier?" She said once she was satisfied with the placement of the blanket.

I stretched out my arm, rubbing the back of my neck. One of my tells that I was uncomfortable. "He's passed out in the truck. He's staying here, too?"

She nodded and Aaron offered to help me bring him in. I stood there a moment, processing.

"Hey, Behemoth, chill. He's going to be on the couch, plus he's gay."

Surprise colored my cheeks. It shouldn't matter. The blonde wasn't my girl. I had no claim on her, and she had made it clear she didn't want a claim on me.

Aaron and I carried Xavier in and placed him on the couch. With one last look at the girl who strutted away with a piece of my soul, I clapped Aaron on the back and left.

My mind was running a million miles an hour. Even though the blonde had run from me, after fragmenting a part of my soul and taking it with her, she had continued to come to the bar. I wanted to believe it was because she wanted to see me, but I knew better.

I also knew my best friend and if Aaron was as serious about his girl as I thought he was, then I would be seeing more of the Firecracker from a few weeks ago.

I couldn't decide if I was excited by the idea, or terrified.

Ronnie

Three

I had not been feeling well, and it couldn't be a hangover. Even though last night I only had one drink, my usual headache was gone, and though I was nauseous, I couldn't actually throw up.

This was literal hell.

Sitting beside the toilet in my small apartment was not how I wanted to start my morning. Especially on my day off. I wanted to go to the new thrift store downtown, and maybe ask Haven to join me.

Instead I sat around, feeling sick to my stomach and scrolling through my phone while Netflix played in the background. I couldn't eat, fear that I was going to puke my guts up kept me from anything from my kitchen.

Other than water. I drank more of it than I think I ever had.

I opened my period tracker, wanting to see what funny quote it would have for me today. Instead it wasn't a quote...

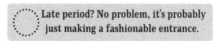
Late period? No problem, it's probably just making a fashionable entrance.

I scrambled up to find my calendar, I never missed a period. It was always on time. Frantically I placed my finger on today's date and counted back to when I should have started.

Fuck.

Five days.

How did I miss my period for five fucking days?

I tried not to panic, but so help me, my brain was in full out, red button panic mode. Grabbing my keys and shoes I stormed out of my apartment to head to Olde Elixr Parlor. Georgie would keep my secret and wouldn't ask me too many questions.

The windows were being scraped to start their holiday season display and my heart flipped. Christmas was my favorite season, everyone in high spirits, red and green posted everywhere.

The bell above the door chimed it's happiness to have a customer, and Georgie's beautiful voice rang out. "Hi! Welcome, let me know if you need anything."

I quickly found the pregnancy test aisle, of course beside it would be condoms. We used one. I know we did, so why am I freaking out?

Maybe with all the excitement going on my period is just...readjusting.

I grabbed two boxes, one pink and one purple. I had to have a second opinion.

"Georgie! It's me!" I hollered.

"Oh Ronnie!" She said, coming around the corner behind the counter. "Oh."

"Could this be our little secret?" I asked, covering the boxes with the brown paper bags they used.

Her face split into a knowing grin. "Of course, dear."

She patted my hand after bagging the two boxes and I bolted out of there, ready to know.

When I got home, I downed a bottle of water and ripped open one of the packages. The pink foil was tough to open. After wrestling with the wrapping I uncapped the stick and let it flow.

The little window against the white immediately started to turn. Absorbing quickly and just as quickly my heart tripled. Agonizingly slowly two pink lines appeared.

Pregnant.

"Oh God," I shrieked and slapped a hand to my mouth to stop the sob from escaping.

My other hand closed down on the porcelain sink to steady my fuzzy head. I splashed water over my face and went to the kitchen to guzzle down more water.

Time for that second opinion.

Ronnie

Four

I'd never considered what life would be like if I had a child. It had never even crossed my mind. I didn't even think I could ever *have* children. My last few doctors also didn't think I could, so how did I find myself in the bathroom of a doula's office with a positive pregnancy test?

That's a good question. One I would also like an answer to.

There's a knock on the door to the little washroom I'd been holed up in much longer than necessary. The lighting was dim, with only one tiny powder blue lamp sitting on a small round table in the mid-center of the room. I guess it's for when people cry because they've found out they're carrying a life, they don't look red and splotchy in the mirror.

"Everything alright Veronica?"

Oh God. She used my full name. I was definitely not going out that door, definitely not giving her my positive pee stick,

and I was most definitely *not* calling my best friend, Bellamy.
She had enough to worry about without me adding to it.

I should probably start by going to my actual doctor, right?
The same one who told me I didn't need to worry about
pregnancy because my uterus was shaped like a heart. I
laughed and told her that's where God placed it, instead of
in my chest.

She didn't think it was funny.

I could hear the woman on the other side speaking to
someone in hushed tones. They were talking about me, I
just knew it, and why wouldn't they? I mean, I walked in
without an appointment, asked for information brochures,
and walked out. That was this morning, and now I'm back,
with an appointment–thank you very much–and I was
chickening out.

"Ver-Ronnie?" Another voice said, choking on my name
to correct herself. "May I come in?"

I nodded, like an idiot. She couldn't see me, or at least I
hoped she couldn't. That would be weird, and super illegal
I thought.

Of course, it was.

The lock snicked and the sound felt like a death sentence,
loud in the silence of my freak-out. A tall woman with
smooth tawny skin slipped into the small room. Braids fell
from her head, much like my boss's wife, Kelly's. Except

they were all one color and lacked the golden jewels Kelly preferred.

Her smile was dazzling, not a wrinkle in sight. There was no way she was in her fifties like the brochure said, she couldn't be much older than my thirty-two. Her lips were painted a dark purple color, she was dressed in jeans and a comfy looking long-sleeve sweater, and her kind eyes were softening around the edges.

"Hi, Ronnie," she started, her voice like melted butter, smooth and strong, yet incredibly gentle. "How are you feeling?"

My mouth opened, damn near dropping to the floor. "Me?" I pointed to my chest, fingernails long since worn down to the nub.

She laughed a little, smiling even more than when she first arrived if it was even possible. "Yes, you. All of these big emotions are hitting you at once. It's got to feel...overwhelming, I'd guess?"

I tried to gather my thoughts because I had a lot of them rattling around in my brain. Where did I start? Do I tell her my medical history? Do I need to call someone to let them know I'm going with another doctor?

Was a doula even a doctor? Was she qualified to birth a baby? Was I?

She reached across the room, her hands slowly gripping my biceps as she gently pushed me onto the little table with the lamp.

"I can see your brain working overtime through your eyes." She closed the toilet lid and sat to face me. "Let me tell you a little more about myself than what you'll find in those brochures." She was waiting for me to give her some signal to move forward, but I continued to stare at her, thoughts churning.

"Okay. I am a licensed obstetrician. Practiced for twenty years, and now I'm also a doula, certified in all fifty states. I've delivered hundreds of babies. The difference between me and your last doctor? I practice natural medicine, but am fully capable of handling medicated cases as well."

"I'm pregnant." It's the first time I'd said it out loud, and it felt foreign rolling off my tongue. The admittance, the acceptance, was peaceful, hanging in the air like an invisible thread waiting to be woven into my life's tapestry.

"Is that what the test said? Or your body?" She nodded to the pregnancy test, where two pink lines shined clear as day, unmistakable.

"I didn't think I could have a baby," I whispered, trying to hold back tears. I wasn't sure I could blame the hormones just yet, but I'd cried more in the past two days than I had in as long as I could remember. "My body isn't right for a baby."

She wrapped her arms around my shoulders and hugged me tight as silent tears tracked paths down my cheeks. "Your body is perfect for your baby." With her rubbing soothing circles on my back I cried harder, harder than I had in a long, long time.

I lifted my head once I felt more in control of my emotions, only to decide a hole is what I shall now live in because my tears stained her nice sweater, and snot began to pour out of my nose. She probably thought I was a train wreck, crying over becoming pregnant when there were women out there who would kill to be in my position.

I was mortified, and mentally chastising myself for all of my ungrateful thoughts. "I'm sorry."

She looked down at her shoulder, the one now sporting a huge wet spot from my freak out, and said, "Oh this? It's the new 'in' fashion, didn't you know?"

We laughed in unison, and I felt a weight lift slightly off my chest. "I need to tell the father." I spit out so quickly I didn't think she heard me.

"That's a great first step. How about we go ahead and do an exam, an ultrasound, and bloodwork to make sure everything is healthy?"

"Yeah, okay." I whispered to myself still not convinced this was real.

Ronnie

Five

I nodded, as if on autopilot letting her guide me up and out of the bathroom. Bright light assaulted my senses after being in the near dark for so long. Then I remembered my pee stick. Dropping the doctor's hand I rushed back in and grabbed the offending device. Holding it up for everyone to see, "Can't forget this."

The nice lady in the front chuckled a little under her breath and the doctor smiled. It occurred to me that I still didn't know her name, because all of the information in the brochures was jumbled up in my brain. I saw framed degrees along the light gray walls as she led me ahead.

Dr. Ashton Sofia Steele.

A giggle burst from my body uninhibitedly. Her initials were A.S.S. Gah I bet kids gave her hell growing up.

She smiled as if she knew what I was thinking. "Sorry," I mumbled, ashamed that was the first thing my mind thought, especially since she'd been nothing but nice to me. She waved her hand dismissing the sentiment.

"Call me Dr. Ass, I know Regina does behind my back."

"I do not!" I heard the front desk lady shout with a laugh.

"She does. But sometimes I deserve it." She whispered behind her hand like we were co-conspirators. "You may also just call me Ashton."

Continuing a few short steps she opened a door to our left, signaling I go in first. The room was sparsely furnished, with the exam table and a television mounted on the wall. There was a rolling chair in the room, that as a child, I had always wanted to sit on but my parents never let me.

C'mon, it *spinned*.

The thought clanged around in my head and heavy emotions I really don't want to deal with today assaulted my already sensitive heart. It was going to be non-existent by the time I called the father. A not so random guy now.

My eyes traced over the room. On the table, there was a paper-like cover laid over top of the leather, and a blue piece of fabric folded and placed near the end.

"If you would, please remove your bottoms and cover yourself with the blue cloth. I'll be right back and we'll get everything taken care of for you."

She left the room, shutting the door with a final snick. I took a deep breath, modesty had never been my middle name, but for the first time since I took my first pregnancy test a little over twenty-four hours ago, it finally felt real.

I refused to get my hopes up though because this shouldn't have been possible, and I don't know if I could survive it if my body hurt my little bean. I undressed from the waist down like Dr. Ass asked, situating my body on the cool cream leather and drapped the blue fabric across my bare legs.

I had to admit this experience was much nicer than the doctor I'd been seeing since Bellamy and I came into town a few years ago.

Ashton-because I should probably stop calling my new doctor "Ass" even if it was her initials-came back, with who I assumed to be Regina in tow. Regina rolled in a cart with all kinds of devices, colors, and tubes, it all tumbled over in my head.

"Regina, you two met earlier. This is Veronica, though she prefers Ronnie." She waved a blue-covered hand and beamed a smile my way.

"Ronnie, Regina will be taking a couple of tubes of blood to test your varying levels, and then we'll get to the ultrasound, is that okay?"

I nodded, unable to really look away from the tray Regina slid out from somewhere on the cart. She arranged a few of the colorful tubes in a row complete with a needle that was attached to the plastic thing for collecting blood through, gauze, alcohol pads, and that blue bungee cord I hated.

I tried not to tense my muscles as Regina started to talk, it wasn't that I was scared of needles, I just didn't particularly like the pain they caused. Which was why I had my one and only tattoo. I liked adventure, and I could never back down from a dare, two things that landed me with a bite mark permanently tattooed on my ankle.

Thanks, bestie.

Regina strapped the rubbery but pinchy cord apparatus around my arm tight, and then poked and prodded at my inner arm for a nice fat vein to bleed. When she was satisfied by the one she'd found, she cleaned the area and slid the needle in. I couldn't hear a word she said. Honestly, I don't think I listened to anything she'd said since she started.

It's a curse really, my thoughts bounced from one thing to the next. If my therapist had anything to say about it, she'd call it my coping mechanism. I'd had to juggle so much on my own from such a young age that jumping from one task to another was learned early on.

The curse really came in handy during wedding season, which for Bellamy and I was all year. I don't know how I got lucky enough to work with my best friend, but I thanked my guardian angel every night before bed that I had her.

The blue fabric shifted as Dr. Ashton positioned herself at my feet. My feet, that she magically moved into stirrups while my mind was elsewhere. Regina smiled like this happened all the time. I looked down at my elbow to see a neat bright green bandage wrapped around gauze to keep my blood from ruining my clothes while it dried.

"Okay." I breathed. Anticipation lit up my stomach, or maybe it was the pop-tart I ate on the way over. Either way, Dr. Ashton was explaining the wicked-looking white wand that couldn't possibly be going where I thought it was.

"What kind of torture device is that?"

I hadn't meant to say it out loud, but I realized my mistake the moment Regina and Ashton burst into laughter.

"We're doing an internal exam. We want to get accurate measurements as soon as possible." Her smooth voice calmed me down, if only a little before she piled lube up on the wand at an alarming rate.

"It may be slightly uncomfortable at first, but I promise it gets better, and it won't take long."

I snorted, that should be the warning label made for some men.

She counted down from three and slowly pushed the device into my body. The screen crackled white and black static for a few seconds while I felt like she played peek-a-boo with the baby.

Baby.

The moment I thought of it, she was pointing at the screen where I could clearly see what a little human looked like in my body. She talked some more about size and weeks, but it all sounded like static to me. I still couldn't believe this was possible.

Could I even carry a baby full-term?

"....six weeks along."

I tried to wrangle my thoughts back into the present, the questions could wait, maybe I could make a list and tackle them one by one...my thoughts stopped at the sound coming out of the machine.

th-wap th-wap th-wap

A rapid muffled sound filled the room as my focus zeroed in on the monitor. Dr. Ashton and Regina were smiling, "That's your baby's heartbeat."

My...what?

"I'm having a baby," I muttered, tears leaked out of the corners of my eyes, dripping down towards my ears in my reclined position. I tore my eyes away from the monitor and focused on the ceiling.

Dr. Ashton removed the wand and quietly left the room so I could clean myself up and get dressed. I did it all in a daze as if I wasn't the one controlling my body.

Regina walked me to another office with a desk, two chairs, and a few plants scattered about. I sat in one of the plush chairs as Regina handed me a bottle of water and a chocolate bar.

I unwrapped the chocolate and ate it in a few bites. As I guzzled the water Dr. Ashton came in with a tiny envelope, rounded the desk, and sat. She was smiling a big bright smile, teeth immaculately straight making her dark lipstick even darker.

"I have your sonogram pictures if you would like to have them." She stated, not quite a question, but not really a statement either.

I reached across the desk and gently grabbed the envelope from her. As I stared at the back of the envelope Dr. Ashton started again. "I know pregnancy is rough, and yours will be a high risk. I'm not saying it's not possible, I'm just asking to take closer care of you."

I nodded, still staring at the sealed envelope.

"When you're ready, I'd like to get you set up on a monthly basis, just to start out. Then as time grows closer we'll start seeing you every three to two weeks."

"Okay."

She stood up when I did and followed me to the front where Regina was talking with another woman whose tummy was so full her belly button poked out through her cute floral top. Her hand rested over the swell of her stomach, like a perch made specifically for her.

Dr. Ashton gripped my shoulders, gently shaking me out of my auto-pilot mode, "Ronnie, I'll have Regina email you our phone numbers, personal too. You call me if you have any issues. We want a healthy momma and baby through this whole process. Don't forget we're here for everything, I mean it."

I nodded. God, it felt like all I had done since I got here was smile and nod. There were tears that wanted to spill and my throat began to burn as I pushed through the glass doors of my new physician's office. The Uber I ordered wasn't here yet, so I sat on the bench located under one of the decorated trees on the sidewalk, and just let the tears fall. I still couldn't believe this was actually happening to me, but I was already tired of crying.

Scrolling through my phone I found Bellamy's contact. If anyone could get me in touch with the father of this baby, it'd be Aaron.

Finn

Six

Weights slammed on metal, grunts echoed through the large space of Wadey Weights. The bright colors of the space that I'd dubbed my second home were randomized shapes on the wall. Splattered against the black mats.

It was like the 90's had thrown-up in here.

I tackled a few more curls and re-racked the weights when I heard my phone ring. Usually I let calls go to voicemail when I was here. It was my safe space, and when my phone rings it's usually not good news.

A number I didn't recognize popped up on the screen. It was a local area code, so I answered. "Hello."

"Finn?" A feminine voice said softly.

"Yeah," I replied, confusion evident in my voice. "Who is this?"

"Ver-", she started and restarted with a hiccup. "Firecracker."

My brows shot up to my hairline, *holy shit*. It's her. "Bellamy's friend?"

"Yeah." She squeaked. "Can you meet me for dinner tonight?"

"Yes." I answered, right way. "I mean, tell me where." I tried to collect myself.

"Billy's Diner?"

"I'll be there, Firecracker." I replied before I hung up.

We had agreed to meet there at six, and the time on my phone said I had about three hours to get myself together.

After rushing through a shower and dressing, I headed to Billy's Chicken Pit. I was early, so I sat in the gravel lot and scrolled through my phone.

Time stood still as I saw her walking into the restaurant, hair curled and blowing in the wind. My heart picked up speed, sweat gathered in my palms. The girl who said no names, knew mine. The girl who said no repeats, called me for a date. The girl who said no strings, well...she had something to say.

To *me*.

I could see it in the way her shoulders straightened when I walked into the little hole in the wall diner. The way her eyes glanced from window to doorway, as if she was waiting to be caught with me a second time.

"Hi." I said, sliding into the booth across from her.

She ducked her head and continued looking anywhere but at me. Her eyes darted around, cheeks growing pale.

"Are you okay?"

"We used a condom, right?" She blurted out, eyes squarely landing on mine.

"Yeah." I answered, confused and more nervous than before. "Why?"

"I'm pregnant."

It took her words a few minutes to actually sink in. Pregnant. Like with a baby? *My* baby? I thought the condom felt funny after we finished, but I couldn't see well enough to know if it had broken.

Well...okay.

"And you think it's mine?"

Her eyes went to slits, "Yes, Finn. It's yours."

"Okay."

"Okay... Okay? That's all you have to say?" Her hands landed on the table with a loud smack. "I'm fucking pregnant." She said between gritted teeth.

"Okay, Firecracker." I said, placing my hands on hers. "We can figure this out."

Her eyes jumped from my hands covering hers to my face. "We can?"

"Of course. Let's start with names."

Her eyes went big, rounded and watery. A waitress brought her a milkshake, it was sweating by the time she finally grasped the straw and took a large sip.

"Veronica Gibson, but everyone calls me Ronnie."

"Finn Hart." I said, keeping my hand as close to hers as possible. I wanted to touch her, to make sure she knew I was here.

"How are you so calm?"

"Oh, I'm freaking the fuck out on the inside." I answered honestly. "And I have a lot of questions."

She nodded, "Me too."

"Where do we start?" I asked, willing to follow her lead.

"I have no idea."

Ronnie

Seven

Ever since I called Finn a week ago, he had been around more and more. We were still figuring out what the hell we were doing, but as of right now. I was just glad he was willing to keep my secret.

I hadn't told my two best friends about the baby. With work and Bellamy learning to love again, it was difficult to find the time, and I wasn't ready to have the conversation yet. My best friend was amazing, I knew she would understand.

Finn has been more than enough to fill my time. We had been talking, and texting, and sending baby things to each other. It's become a nice surprise everytime I see a notification pop up on my phone.

Little butterflies erupted every time I saw him, and I thought for a fleeting moment about my rules.

His name flashed on my screen and I answered, "Hello, baby daddy."

"Ugh," he groaned, "why do you insist on calling me that?"

"Because you are." I sing-songed, "And because it makes me laugh, imagining your face everytime I say it."

"Ha-Ha." He said in a mocking tone. "What are you doing tonight?"

"I'm actually heading to Xavier's for game night. Why?"

"Can I come over after? I've got something to show you."

"Ominous..." I answered, "But I'll bite, I'll let you know when I'm home."

"Promises, promises." He tisked, and ended the call.

The Uber to Xavier's was quiet, the driver girl didn't talk, and I didn't either. When we arrived I offered her a cash tip and slipped out of the car. I was ready to just relax after the past few events as of late. We'd all been busy with Haven and Adrian lately, it was nice to have time for just us.

His house was always decorated to the nines. Pumpkins and wreaths, twigs and miniature hay bales dotted the front porch. Against the blue of his house it was the perfect fall palette.

Xavier threw open the front door and pulled me into his cozy home. His twin, Penelope, was perched on the edge of his couch.

"Oh my! Penelope! I didn't know you were in town." I squeezed her up in a hug and Xavier set about throwing dishes around.

"I made my woo-woos!" Xavier hollered, like his house was ten times bigger than it actually was.

"We hear you, old queer one!" Penelope shouted back.

Her sass always elicited laughter, and her loving endearment of his sexuality never failed to be funny. He loved it, like his own personal moniker. He brought us two iridescent glasses of pink liquid and winked before getting into a heated discussion with Penelope. I swapped out my alcohol for water. No way was I taking any more chances with our baby.

Xavier and I gossiped about Bell and Aaron, all good things, of course we had to fill Penelope in. Especially if she was staying in town after finishing school.

When Bellamy and Aaron got there, the place heated up with fun quips and equally funny trash talk. We played round after round of games, ate and just enjoyed each other's company.

Penelope had gotten a new game, one with a wheel of letters and cards. The alphabet was mixed in black toggles around the blue device, Xavier read the directions and we set about figuring out who would start.

Category cards ranged from 'fruits' to 'something hard', which made us all a giggle. Xavier, unable to help himself, picked the category labeled 'something hard' and hit the timer. As it clicked we went around the table shouting and laughing, holding our sides.

Xavier slammed down the letter P and hollered "PENIS".

Bellamy hit the letter D and yelled "DICK".

When it came to me, I cleverly pressed the letter A and called out "ASS".

We all doubled over, because I loved a good firm ass. You could catch me talking about Henry Cavil's ass any day of the week.

"You dirty girly!" Xavier winked.

"You said penis!" I countered as Penelope and Bellamy swiped their eyes with their sweaters. "We all know who the pervert is here."

That sent us all into another laughing fit, we ate snacks and passed around life stories to catch up.

Bellamy dropped news about her parents, and I felt guilty for not sharing my secret.

It wasn't that I didn't trust them, because I did. With my life.

I just wasn't ready to answer questions I was still trying to answer myself.

After Bellamy and Aaron left, I followed, letting Finn know I was on my way back to my apartment.

I was excited for whatever this surprise was.

Despite the strings.

Ronnie

Eight

He was waiting by his truck when the Uber driver dropped me off.

"Why didn't you call me? I would have driven you." His voice was gruff, his hair was down and wavy over his shoulders. I remembered running my hands through it once, the soft strands were cool against the heat searing between us.

"And how would I explain that to my two besties who wouldn't be able to leave it alone?"

He nodded his head in thought, obviously thinking about how that would play out. "Fair."

"So where's my surprise?" I asked, hopping up onto the curb to gain a little height.

"I don't remember promising you a surprise." He said, sneakily.

"You absolutely did!" I said, playfully swatting at his crossed arms.

He caught my wrists in his big hands and pulled me in so my chest was against his. He planted a kiss on my cheek and ushered me inside.

"Come on, we can't have you getting a cold now."

I rolled my eyes, but relented. I unlocked the door and walked into my personal bubble. Glancing around the room, my eyes landed on the couch where Finn and I have had many conversations.

His hands landed on my hips as the door closed behind him. He twirled me around, and I looped my arms around his neck. Resting my head on his shoulder we stood there for a moment. Just listening to his heart beat in time with mine.

He gave me a squeeze and released me.

"I'm gonna change, make yourself at home."

I threw my hair up into a bun and put on my most comfortable clothes. A silky sleep short and an oversized t-shirt.

He was seated on the couch, legs splayed wide like men do when they get comfortable.

"Okay, the suspense is killing me!" I said, unable to hide my excitement. I joined him on the couch, on my knees hovering over him.

"Alright. Alright." He said, digging his phone from his pocket. He swiped through a few pictures before settling on a screenshot of a high rise not too far from here.

"What's this?" I asked. I had an apartment, and as far as I knew Finn had a house in the city.

"It's my new place, it's closer than my condo now, so I can be here for all of your appointments and stuff."

My eyes began to water, and my bottom lip poked out. It was the nicest thing he could have done. "You don't have to move closer." Something so big could only mean that he was serious about this. About us.

"I know I don't have to, but I want to. It will make everything easier, especially when the baby comes."

I was relieved that he wanted to, that it was all his idea and I didn't have to bring it up. I didn't want to ask him to move in with me, but nights with a baby could be long, and tiring.

"Maybe we could..." He began, "Spend a few nights together, before the baby comes?"

Getting attached to him was a bad idea. I already felt like my resolve was slipping. I looked forward to his texts, calls, even his company. Spending nights together would lead to more feelings, and scary things.

"I don't know..." I started.

"You don't have to have an answer now." He interrupted. "Just, maybe next time I bring it up, could you try not to look like it's the last thing on earth you want to do?" He laughed, and I tried not to be embarrassed that he knew me well enough to see the terror on my face. "Hurts a guy's ego."

"I'm sorry." I said, covering my face and leaning back against the couch.

"No, no, no." He said, prying my hands away from my face. "You don't get to hide those crimson cheeks."

"Yes I do!" I screeched as he started tickling my sides.

I was breathless by the time he finished his assault. He was draped over me, his arms caging me in, his biceps brushed my cheeks.

His legs were tangled with mine, and I felt my stomach tumble. The way he was looking at me made me want to melt into a puddle.

Our eyes connected and we stayed there, suspended in "what if's" and "could we's"?

"Kiss me, pretty boy." I said, barley above a whisper.

His eyes stayed on me until his lips were a hair's breadth away from mine. Feather soft he brushed his lips against my mouth, fire ignited in my veins, and I pulled him to me. His hard body lined up in all the right places.

His mouth moved over mine, exactly how I wanted. Demanding and in charge, hard, yet tender. We stayed that way for a while, using each other's lips, teeth, and tongue.

"Firecracker." He moaned as my hands began to roam. "Rules."

"None tonight." I whispered.

He pulled back and searched my eyes, I wanted to feel tonight. I wanted to pretend that we could be in love. That he was the man I chose to break my rules over.

"*Please*." I whimpered and circled my hips, creating delicious friction.

One word and his resolve broke, he moved my neck with a tattooed hand placing me exactly where he wanted. His greedy hands roamed and groped everywhere and nowhere I needed.

When I growled in frustration he chuckled and lifted himself off me. He bent down, sliding his hands under my body to move me off the couch. He carried me to the bed and stripped me of my clothes. Completely bare to him, he bit into his bottom lip and quickly undressed.

His hands wrapped around my ankles and he spread them wide, cool air pebbled my slick skin.

"God, Ronnie."

It felt good to hear him say my name, and not just some nickname he chose in haste.

My. Name.

Finn

Nine

She flushed under my words. Her beautiful skin glowed with praise.

Her pussy was soaked, and I wanted nothing more than to have a feast. She wiggled against my hands, rubbing her thighs together, hiding my prize.

I swatted the side of her ass, and she gasped.

"Did you just...spank me?"

"Be a good girl and let me eat this pretty pussy, or I'll do it again." I grumbled, moving over her legs, running my hands along her shins and squeezing her thighs. Using the pads of my fingers to tease her open, I groaned at the feel of her arousal.

She whimpered and groaned, wiggling closer to me.

Slowly I licked her cunt, flattening my tongue and going painfully slow. I circled her clit, making her shift and raise her hips.

"More."

I bit the inside of her thigh, and she cried out.

"Be patient." I warned.

I took my time, I licked and sucked, driving her out of her mind with the feeling of my fingers working her nipples, and my tongue fucking her pussy. She made these sounds that drove me wild, keens and wails of pleasure, but no release.

Grabbing handfuls of her ass I pulled her cunt to my face, and devoured her. Shoving my two middle fingers into her wetness and curling them just right. She bucked and fussed, jumbled words tumbled from her mouth.

"Finn, I'm gonna…" She couldn't finish before her climax hit its peak and her thighs gripped my head like a vice.

I didn't stop, continuing to gently lap at her as she rode waves of ecstasy.

She went limp, legs straight out and she shivered as I ran the calloused tips of my fingers over the skin of her stomach, her breasts.

I pinched her nipples and lined myself up.

"You ready, Firecracker?"

She nodded, quickly coming down from her high. I eased into her, and she cried out, nails digging into my back.

"*Fuck.*"

Gripping the sheets near her head I pulled out and thrust back into her, over and over before lifting one of her legs and hooking her knee over my elbow. Her body moved perfectly in sync with mine as we grinded together and created the most delicious friction.

When she was shaking and screaming out her second orgasm under me, I lost it. Thrusting with abandon until I pulled out, flipped her over, and came all over her beautiful ass.

The sight alone had me ready for round two, but I knew by the way her breaths puffed in and out that she'd be asleep soon. Pregnancy had taken its toll recently, and she'd been heading to bed sooner rather than later these days.

I walked into the bathroom to find a washcloth and start the tub. When the water was warm enough I soaked the rag and squeezed out as much as I could before heading back toward where Ronnie was lazily smiling.

Wiping my mess off her bouncy ass had me biting my lip and forcing myself to relax. I needed to get her cleaned up and in bed before she fell asleep.

"Come on, Firecracker." I said, wrapping her up in her sheet and walking her to the bathroom. "I'll wash, okay."

She nodded, and sat in the tub I had filled with her bottle of bubbles. The scent of berries clung to the air as I washed her hair, making sure to scrub her scalp the way I've seen in my sister's self help blogs.

Soaping up a rag I washed her body, making sure to be extra careful around her sensitive parts. When I was done I pulled the plug and changed her sheets.

It was a quick job, but it would do.

Wrapping her up in a towel I dried off her body and hair the best I could before letting her pass out in bed. I stayed with her for a while, stroking her hair and watching her sleep.

She looked peaceful when her walls were down, almost like she didn't have a care in the world. But I knew her rules, and I prayed she didn't regret this in the morning.

Finn

Ten

The voicemail popped up as I was unlocking my front door. I hated not being able to answer since I left my watch here and my hands were full of gym shit.

I knew it was Ronnie by the ringtone I'd chosen. *'In da club'* by 50 Cent, she hated it, and that was all that I needed to keep it.

"Finn," Her voice cracked, and she sniffled. "I-I'm bleeding, I don't know what's happening." She hiccuped again and my heart hit the floor. I stood there, like a fucking statue. Instead of racing to her, I panicked. "...we hurt our baby."

The last few words she uttered registered, between her sobbing and choking. I could hear how scared she was, and if I hurt our baby...if I was the reason we lost our child...I couldn't take it.

I packed a bag of clothes, leaving everything else behind.

"Hi, mom."

I shouldn't have driven almost eight hours away to hide. I should have faced my demons, instead I'm standing on my parent's front step staring at my mother who I must have woken up from bed.

"Oh, honey." She said, looping her arms around my body like she would when I was younger.

Tears come then, in torrents down my face. I can't do this. I don't know why I thought I could. I'm not good for anyone, not reliable, not accountable, and I've never had any responsibilities.

How could I trap Ronnie into a life with me? She deserves someone who isn't a fuck up. A party boy.

"I can't do it." I hiccuped, the sound was between a sob and sneeze. "I can't chain her to me for eighteen years."

"Come in here." She said as she pulled me into the house I hadn't visited in a long time. The same house that saw many of these breakdowns. I wasn't the same person I was when I left, but I'm not the best man to raise a fucking baby with an incredible woman.

She made two cups of coffee and sat them on the low table in front of their couch. My thoughts swirled like technicolor, jumbled and messy as I tried to explain to her what happened.

"This girl...woman." I corrected, "She's incredible, wild and funny. She's going to be an amazing mother."

"A woman?" One of her eyebrows raised. I forgot I hadn't even told her about Ronnie in the first place.

"Ronnie, I met her at Giselle's bar." I wanted to tell her the whole story, but telling your mother you fucked a stranger in your sisters club and got her pregnant wasn't something I wanted to share. "We...spent some time together."

"Some time..." My mother repeated, a smirk graced her lips.

"We slept together," God this was excruciating. But I needed her advice, I needed her to tell me what to do. "Mom, I swear it was consensual."

She laughed and tapped my knee, "So this woman has you in a bit of a panic?"

"A bit? I drove almost eight hours for advice from my *mother* for fucks sake!" I had to calm down, I didn't want to yell at her. "She's pregnant, and it's mine. I didn't notice the condom broke, it was dark. I was riding the high of getting off with a hot woman who'd been noticing me for a while"

"I've been hanging out with her for the past couple of weeks." Tears start to flow again. "She's amazing, mom.

Unlike any woman I've ever met. And I'm the piece of shit who got scared and ran." I had to pause and inhale a shaky breath. "I came here without my phone. I have no way to contact her, and even if I did, I have no idea what I'd say to her."

"I fucked up, and I don't know how to fix it." I looked into my mom's eyes and asked, "How do I fix this mom? How do I prove to her I can do this?"

She grasped my hands in hers, the softness of her skin soothed a part of my inner child. Calm washed over me, and I realized I was more tired than I thought.

"I think you need to work on Finn first."

I nodded, what the hell else was I going to do at damn near midnight?

"I'm sorry I'm such a fuck up."

"We all make mistakes," she said, her eyes glossed over for a moment before it was gone. "It's what we do to make it right that counts. It's the ways in which we choose to show up that matter. Actions over words, sweet boy."

I let her guide me up the stairs and into a bed that I swore I'd never come back to. The same bed I had my heart broken in, experienced my first panic attack in, and lost my virginity in.

"In the morning we'll make a plan, okay?" She patted my side and I felt the mattress shift under her slight weight. She sat with me, allowing me the space to feel whatever it was that I needed to in that moment until the tears slowed. She got up and walked out, shutting the door behind her.

I wondered if Ronnie knew I was gone, if she was going to hate me forever for leaving. I drifted off to sleep wondering what she was feeling, and hating myself just a little bit more knowing if she was half as scared as me, then I had some serious groveling to do.

The next morning I woke to the smell of pancakes and maple syrup. I followed my nose to the kitchen and found both of my parents, sitting at the breakfast table while a chef prepared their breakfast.

My mother looked as beautiful as she always did, her makeup was done, clothes tailored in precise lines. My father drank his coffee as he read whatever sports magazine he was into nowadays. His rich dark hair mirrored mine, thick, but cut in a wave on top of his head.

"Good morning, Finn." He said, his tone was light almost like he was genuinely happy to see me.

"Morning." I grumbled. I swiped a cup of coffee and a plate of pancakes.

"Your mother filled me in." He began, "I hope you're not thinking of neglecting to raise that child."

"I'm not father material," I hung my head. My father wasn't a vindictive man, he was harsh when he needed to be, but I knew he loved me. That was something I could always count on.

"Finn, you absolutely could be." My mother tucked a strand of my hair behind my ear, but I shrugged her off, refocusing on my father.

"Dad, I don't know the first thing about being a father. I'm scared." I couldn't keep ignoring the way my heart beat double time when I thought of Ronnie. "I think I love her."

"Then you can figure it out." My mother said, gripping my hand and giving it a squeeze.

I shook my head, "It's not that simple. She doesn't do relationships."

My dad scoffs, "Then you'll have to change her mind, son."

"What's she like?" My mom asked.

Damn, how could I describe Ronnie? I couldn't put her in a box, she was so much of everything that I couldn't pin it down.

"She's...incredible." I laughed, "She's tall and blonde, and has the most beautiful blue eyes I've ever seen."

My mother made a sound of adoration, and my cheeks went hot when I noticed her eyes were wide and glassy.

"Mom," I groaned.

"I've never heard you speak about anyone like that. With such open affection. It makes me happy."

Her strong willed, easy going nature was something I didn't know I needed in my life. A fast paced Firecracker who didn't let anything bother her. Just thinking about going back to her had my lips rising into a smirk.

"I hope one day y'all can meet her."

My mom patted my hand. "We will."

Finn

Eleven

I sat in my old room after showering off all the previous day's grime. I needed to figure this out, to get a clear head so when I saw Ronnie again I would be less anxious and more helpful.

A knock came on the door frame, followed by my father's deep rasp. "Come to lunch with me today?"

"Sure." I nodded.

I trailed him down the steps and into their garage where he unlocked his SUV for me to climb into. Mom's car was already gone, she was a busy lady after all. With all the charity work she had been doing I was surprised she even stayed this morning for coffee.

We didn't speak as he drove us to their country club, we parked and he waved to a few men also dressed in golf attire on our way into the building. The hostess eyed us both with appreciation.

Before Ronnie, I would have openly flirted with her, but now it felt wrong. Even though I knew Ronnie wasn't ready for a relationship, I still felt a connection with her. Like our lives were destined to be interwoven somehow.

I didn't want anything to mess that up.

She walked us to my father's favorite low table with plush leather covered chairs. The men around us had cigars smoking and liquor flowing.

Ah, to be retired.

"Son, I wanted to talk to you without your mother around." My dad said after the waitress had come by to take our orders. "This woman, she's not asking you for anything?"

"No." I lowered my brow, immediately on edge.

"Good. I just want to make sure, before you go through all of this, that she's not after your inheritance."

"Ronnie isn't like that." I couldn't help the way I defended her. Even though Ronnie never asked me for anything other than emotional support, I knew, deep in my soul, that my money had nothing to do with it.

"I had to ask." He took a sip of his drink, "When this one is born, you'll understand."

"*This one?*"

"Finny Boy, I have no doubt that once you have one, you'll want three more." He chuckled and I blanched. "You have so much love to give, that you'll be surprised at the way your heart wants to burst the second that baby is born."

"I'm scared."

"I know, and that's okay."

"I can't keep running away from this, or she'll never let me be a part of our kid's life, or hers."

"So you'll work hard on yourself with Dr. Fitz, and then you can go back to her and never let go." His look was sincere, "we'll be here when you need us. Especially those first few months."

"Thank you."

I didn't know what else to say, we had never been the share your feelings type of father and son duo.

We spent the rest of the meal talking about the changes in our lives and catching up. It was refreshing and I found my anxiety lifting more and more by the second.

"Before we close out our last session I want to commend you on all of your hard work." Dr. Fitz had been my therapist when I was a teenager, going through body image battles.

It's why I worked out so much, I'd been a tall and lanky teen who was bullied relentlessly throughout all of middle school, and then one day my mother brought me to Dr. Fitz. He wasn't the stuffy type of doctor I thought he would be. He was kind and listened to everything I told him. That first session I poured everything out. Word vomit flowed out of me, all while he simply sat and listened.

He didn't take notes on a legal pad like I'd seen in movies, and I didn't lie down like it either.

Although, the couch he had in his office was most certainly comfortable. He also hadn't redecorated since I'd been here last.

His black hair was shot through with silver now, and a gold band winked in the light on his finger. We caught up the first time I came back a few weeks ago, and it was nice. Like a palate cleanse I wasn't aware I needed.

"Thank you." I nodded and crossed my ankle over my knee.

"I know you will give that woman and baby the best version of you. Sometimes you may put too much pressure on yourself and think that you're failing. Hell, I've failed more times than I'd like to admit. But those perceived failures allow us to grow and break out of our molds." His hands were always moving, his button up was rolled to his elbows he'd done it so much. "And remember, if you ever need me, call. I may not be able to see you in person, but I will always make time for you."

We shook hands and he hugged me before I left his office. I'd always felt a kinship to Dr. Fitz, he was like an uncle I didn't know I'd been missing.

Mom and I spent the next couple of days attending a few pregnancy classes, which I do not recommend. Many awkward conversations were had. I think I may have even been propositioned by one of the women. It was...strange to say the least.

Either way, I wanted to be prepared for when I went back. I wanted to prove to Ronnie that I could be just as invested as she had to be, and to start, I was going to make sure she was okay and our baby was still healthy.

But first I needed to prove to myself that I wasn't a quitter, and that I deserved her love.

Congratulations

Your baby is the
size of a lime.

Ronnie

Twelve

It had been a month since I had last heard from Finn.

A whole month of no communication. He didn't answer my calls, texts, or anything. Didn't tell me he'd gone anywhere, or had plans.

Nothing.

So naturally, Bellamy became my rock. Even though I waited to tell her, she understood.

A lot could happen in a month, and I had got a lot to do today, so I didn't have time to worry about all the things plaguing my thoughts. I especially didn't have time for Finn to be calling me. I hit decline for the second time today and marched into the place I'd called home for the past decade, Fixin' To I Do.

The place that had nurtured all of my dreams, and my best friend, Bellamy's. We were the best wedding planners this side of the Mason Dixon, and now our boss had officially handed the keys to the kingdom over to Bell and I.

Holly-Jay and her partner, Kelly, offered us the Tennessee location when we did Haven's wedding in December, hard to believe it was just a little over a month ago. Since Bell met the love of her life, Aaron, Xavier had a business of his own here, and then my current situation with Finn and the baby, it just didn't make sense to move.

We were the bosses now, which I found comical. I could barely keep myself together most days, so having employee's was wild.

"There she is!" Bell said as I casually made my way into the building for the first time as co-owner.

"I'm not late!" I said with as much pep as I could muster after another night of little to no rest.

"Our new couple doesn't get here for another few minutes." Bell laughed, "I just want to check on my favorite tiny human." She pushed off from the wall she was leaning on to lightly place her hands over my stomach. I wasn't showing enough for people to know I was three months pregnant, small blessings really.

Although if anyone had seen our article in Southern Homes, they must have assumed I'd just gotten a pudge and moved on. I hadn't announced my pregnancy to the world yet.

Hell, I hadn't even met Finn's family. But his mother found a way to contact me through that very same article.

I had been dodging her since I still wasn't convinced to give Finn another chance.

It's not that I didn't want my baby to have a relationship with her or his father, or Finn's family. It just scared me to think about inviting all of those people into our life, only to have them cruelly ripped away. And in the same thought, Finn and I just didn't make sense. He was a party boy, a trust fund baby that had little to no desire to do anything productive.

Thoughts surface, images of me holding our baby and sobbing because he'd left again imprisoned my mind. I knew my heart wouldn't survive him choosing to leave a second time.

I couldn't forget my momentary lapse in judgment when I felt my rules beginning to disappear, much like how he disappeared weeks after we became friends, well, more like friends who fuck.

I knew I wasn't the model mother, since I'd been known to party too hard. Now though, it's like a switch turned off in my brain. I no longer wanted to party and get drunk, instead I wanted to enjoy all the time I could with my friends, outside of work of course.

Bellamy was my best bitch, my ride or die, she'd been with me since college. Two outcasts with very different stories, we had immediately meshed. I'd never say that to her, she remembers things a little differently, of course. Once we moved here we made fast friends with Xavier. He was the gay best friend we never saw coming, and his twin sister Penelope just moved back into town. My little crew and I could handle anything, and I didn't want to open my circle further. As far as I was concerned I had everyone I needed already.

"Hello, Veronica." Bell's fiancé, Aaron said coming from the back door of the shop. He wrapped his arms around Bellamy and gently pulled her away from my body. "Already crowding her space, Sunshine?"

Bell swatted his arm, "I would never." She said with a healthy dose of sarcasm.

We laughed, knowing if I were anyone else Bell would never willingly touch my small bump.

The jingle from the bell above our door chimed, and with it the arrival of our newest couple. The bride extended her hand to me as introductions were made. Even though we already knew their names and had a 'vision' for the wedding, it was nice to have faces to pull the whole thing together.

Stacey seemed like a pretty laid back bride, and her fiancé just looked bored. Which was normal, most men typically didn't care what went into the planning. Give them their outfit, time and place, they would be there. No muss, no fuss.

"Thank you both for accepting our application. I saw the Macemore-Scott wedding and knew that I couldn't have anyone else plan my wedding." Stacey's honey eyes lit up, painted pink lips never losing their smile.

"We loved getting to know you both in the letter, and look forward to the next few months together." I said automatically.

We started taking applications instead of using our contact us page. I had thought we were busy after the Southern Homes magazine did a spotlight feature on us, but since Haven Macemore's wedding we had been swamped in requests. Now, instead of charging an exorbitant amount of money, taking all of the weddings we could. We chose brides based on their wants, needs, vision, and most importantly their letter about their partner.

A few letters brought us to tears, Stacey's was one of them. She met Garrett while volunteering at an animal shelter. She was starting over after a particularly bad relationship and wasn't ready for anything serious. But Garrett kept coming around, and eventually wore her resolve down.

The details were sweet, and so, Bell and I decided they would be the best couple to start with after the transition.

Aaron's cell rang and he excused himself, as the door chimed again and another man who looked striking like the groom entered. Garrett and the newcomer slapped backs and smiled, "The prodigal son returns!"

The man laughed, a light scoff that made him seem shy. "It's good to see you too, brother."

Garrett turned to us and introduced his brother as Eli. He had a strong jaw, chiseled cheeks I would die for, and full lips that I was sure many women had swooned over. But his eyes were the real stunner. Framed in dirty blond lashes and prominent eyebrows, his ice blue irises popped against his beige skin.

"It's nice to meet you all." Bell began while I stared at Eli unabashedly. "We can start in the green room just down the hall." They all filed forward, following Bell past our offices into the back room that served as our meeting headquarters.

Eli paused and turned back towards me. "My soon to be sister-in-law talks a lot about you and your friend. I just hope you're worth it."

He didn't say it like a threat, more like doubt, and that just wouldn't do. I stepped forward to stop him and ask exactly what he meant by that. Placing my hand on his chest I was surprised to find it well muscled.

The doorbell went off again, Eli and I both turned, finding a hulk of a man standing in the waiting area, looking completely out of place with his muscles and tattooed arms.

His scowl went feral when he spotted my hand on Eli's chest.

"Finn."

Finn

Thirteen

There she was.

She had been avoiding my calls like I was the damn plague itself come back to haunt her.

"Ronnie." I replied, my voice deep but even. The guy standing between us looked between the two of us once before excusing himself. I couldn't help but scan her from head to toe. Two times wasn't enough in my book, but this woman had 'rules'.

She never had sex with the same man twice. *Until me.*

Aaron pumped Bellamy for all the information he could and what little I knew, Ronnie didn't do relationships. Hadn't in a long time.

I smirked, even though I knew it pissed her off. "New friend?"

"No." She said, and turned on her heel. All I had to do was take two steps and I was in her path.

"What do you mean 'no'?" I asked. She sighed and flipped her phone around to show me her missed call notifications. From my mother, I raise my brows in question.

"I'm not announcing my pregnancy in a magazine article, and you don't get to show up now and demand anything from me." She was practically scolding me.

"I wasn't going to ask you to." I knew my mother was planning something, she was so excited, I just didn't know what since she hadn't thought to let me know. Running my hands through my admittedly unkempt hair I continued, "I want to come to your appointments Ronnie, and I'm tired of you pretending I don't exist."

It was her turn for her brows to skyrocket. Which would have pissed me off, if I didn't have a stellar track record with being in control of my temper.

"I'm not pretending, Finn." Her hands covered her stomach and she looked away from me. "You weren't there."

Her words crushed the beating organ inside of my chest, I knew I'd fucked up. I *knew* I did. I just hoped she'd give me another chance. After I stalled in the doorway of my condo, completely at a loss on how to help her, I knew I had a lot of work to do on my own. The timing wasn't perfect, fuck if it wasn't the worst time, but I couldn't be a good partner, and father if I didn't get my shit together.

So that's what I did.

"Ronnie, please." I plead. I'd get on my knees right in front of this woman if I had to.

She shook her head and moved around me. I let her, because I knew she had clients waiting and I was a little scared of Bellamy.

Her heels clacked on the wood floors they had installed over the Christmas holiday as I watched her walk into the room with that guy from before. I hoped for his sake; the surfer looking guy was the groom.

I walked toward the office Bellamy used now, hoping to find my best friend, Aaron. Sure enough, he was sitting behind her desk working on something at her computer. Maybe part of our security company proposals for future clients.

We both needed career direction. Aaron, because he'd left the Marines the year before last, and I...well, I'd never really had any direction to start with. He convinced me to try private security with him after his successful gig Holly-Jay, his sister, offered.

The same one that brought him the love of his life, Bellamy.

Him and I came up with a plan; I would foot the initial start-up costs with the money my grandparents left me for sixty percent of the company. Until it became profitable for more than a year on its own. Now he'd wrangled me into self-defense classes and training courses to become a working man, just like him.

It wasn't that I'd always been aimless, I'd just never found anything worth settling down for. When Ronnie had called me all those weeks ago to tell me she was pregnant, and it was mine, I hadn't known what to do. I did now, I just wished she'd let me.

"Hey man!" Aaron said as I settled into a chair.

I made a noncommittal noise as the cushion molded to my back. Bellamy had pretty good taste. Everything was redone when Ronnie and Bellamy took over the South Carolina site for Fixin' To I Do.

Now, instead of the bright airy it once was. The office was dark but professional. A delicate balance my sister would love.

"What's up?" Aaron asked, his green eyes pierced mine. His fingers stopped clicking on the keyboard and he leaned back.

"Who's that guy Ronnie was talking to?" I asked him.

He grinned, "Groom's brother."

I nodded and leaned forward on my chair placing my elbows on my knees.

"We need to go back to that building and check out the wiring, I got an email from our contractor that we had some options to decide on before the weekend." Aaron said.

I glanced at him and nodded, I didn't want to talk business now. I wanted to get Ronnie alone and have a long overdue conversation.

"How has she been?"

"Good, I guess." Aaron sighed and leaned back into the chair, "you know I don't want to be the middleman between you and Ronnie."

I had the good sense to look ashamed. It wasn't fair to put one of my best friends in the middle of my mess, but I really wanted to know. God knew Ronnie wasn't about to spill her guts to me, and damn it if I didn't totally understand her for it. It still stung.

"Right. I'm sorry, man." I wanted to pull my hair out, a not so subtle sign of my discomfort. Aaron nodded and we agreed to meet tomorrow afternoon to look at the building with our contractor.

The gym was my safe space. I'd been coming here since I was about fifteen, lacking confidence. Not that I had much of it now, I mocked internally. I'd trained hard, tried so many different diets, but it wasn't easy to maintain perfect obliques. Even though that wasn't at all why I kept training.

Working out kept my mind occupied when I had too many unanswered questions rolling around in my head.

Especially since that phone call. The one that blew up my life, without even trying. I wasn't proud of disappearing on Ronnie after we had spent so much time getting to know each other. I could only guess all the things she probably went through. I'd been reading more pregnancy and baby books, and searching for houses, things I never thought I would do.

I wanted to take care of Ronnie and the baby both. I couldn't do that if I wasn't prepared, and I needed to prove to Ronnie that I was one hundred percent prepared to be a dad. Not *just* a father.

Ronnie

Fourteen

I should have known he'd show up. I hadn't returned any of his many calls, and now his mother was calling and texting all hours of the day. I didn't mind Joline, she was nice and never once called me a gold digger for accidentally getting pregnant with her rich son's child.

Possibly because I wrote him off after he failed to show up for the third appointment I invited him to, and he never answered my frantic phone calls during the scariest moment of my life.

I should have known better than to expect a party boy like Finn to show up for me and this baby. He didn't want this, hell, it had taken me a long few weeks to come to terms with it myself.

Now, though? I wouldn't change a thing. Other than the sickness, that could go any time and I would throw a celebration.

Him showing up while I was talking to Eli and seeing the barely concealed panic on his face though, that was cosmic bliss. Because even though I didn't believe in an eye for an eye, at least he was feeling a fraction of what I felt when he ghosted.

Finn knew I didn't date, so the feeling was short lived. I could have turned up on the flirting, really punched Finn in the gut. I learned a long time ago that I could only rely on myself for things I cared about, my heart included.

But something in me just couldn't. Seeing his eyes round and flatten in a matter of seconds made me feel like I had done something wrong.

Should I have felt that way? No.

I couldn't help it though. Something about the way his features pinched when we spoke briefly in the hall made my stomach tie itself into knots.

"Ronnie can take point on that." I heard Bellamy say, turning the conversation my way. Shit. I hadn't been paying attention, too busy agonizing over a big tattooed jerk.

"Of course!" I said, brightening my smile just enough so they hopefully wouldn't ask questions.

"Ronnie is the best when it comes to wedding dress selections." Bellamy beamed, full of pride, and subtly sending me a hint.

I smiled back at her and hid my rosy face from our clients. I didn't usually get embarrassed, but knowing Bell had caught on to my mental absence made me feel like a shitty friend and co-owner.

"It's settled then." The groom stated, standing up and dragging his fiancé with him.

"We look forward to the itinerary being sent over!" The bride called over her shoulder as her fiancé guided her out.

Bell and I looked at each other, mirrored concern splashed across our faces.

Eli, the groom's brother, chuckled under his breath. "He gets a little...hangry sometimes." He flipped his phone around for us to see a text thread on his phone between him and his brother. Sure enough, the last text was from ten minutes ago asking when 'the hens' would stop blabbing so he could eat.

Bell and I both started laughing, our concern washed away.

"Seriously, thank you for choosing to take them on," he started, eyeing both Bell and I. "They haven't had an easy relationship, but they deserve this."

"That's sweet." I said at the same time Bell makes a 'yuck' face. I kicked her under the table to rearrange her facial muscles before he saw and said something to his brother.

Eli stood, prompting Bell and I to follow and see him out the door. I searched the empty waiting room for any signs of Finn. Not sure if I was hoping he had stayed or gone.

Bellamy leaned against the wall across from the door, arms folded, eyes casually assessing me. "He left."

I sighed. Because ain't that the damn truth. They always leave.

"Here's a thought." She said, tapping her chin with her finger. "Why don't you talk to the behemoth?"

"We both know why that's a really bad idea."

"No. I know why *you* think it's a bad idea. But would Finn agree?"

The understanding look in her hazel eyes reminded me that Bellamy loved me. Tears lined my lashes, pregnancy hormones could suck it. I was already an emotional person, and now anytime anything happened...boom, flood gates activate.

I licked my lips and started toward my office, hoping the tears would absorb back into my body by the time Bell caught up. She was not a fan of walking fast.

"Look, I know I'm the last person who should be giving dating advice–"

"We're giving dating advice?" Aaron strolled out of Bellamy's office, his hand brushed hers in a small but efficient gesture of their affection.

She tilted her head up so she could look at him, "Maybe adulting advice would be more accurate."

He laughed, "Well, in that case, you are most definitely not accredited."

She swatted his arm but continued, "Have a conversation with him. Finn fucked up, I agree. But people can surprise you."

I couldn't find my tongue to continue the conversation. Too many emotions and thoughts took up all the space I had left in my brain.

"Just try." Aaron said as he gripped Bell's hand and pulled her into her office, giving me some semblance of peace.

I only had a few things I needed to finish up before I could leave. I let that take over the space in my brain, and worked on autopilot. I couldn't clear my head of the mess but I could at least pause it. A factory reset, if you will, for my feelings.

Bell left a few minutes ago, locking the front door and hollering at me to be safe. Soon after I received a text.

Bell ♥   Aaron said to remind you to use the back door when you leave. 👀

We didn't use that entrance a lot because the door stuck, but when I was here alone I liked to feel safe locked in here.

Tell him I said I will.

Gathering all the papers on my desk I sorted them into order of importance and left them for tomorrow Ronnie to deal with. As I made my way toward the back door, I turned off all the lights, wiggling the back door just enough so it slid open easily.

The chilly air bit my nose as I made sure to lock the door behind me before starting off for my apartment. I really needed to invest in a car, especially since my stomach would only get bigger with time.

I traveled the sidewalks, admiring the sparkly lights left over from Christmas and New Year's celebrations. Our sleepy little town was slow to recover from holiday events.

A car slowly crawled past me, nothing too out of the ordinary since the speed limit through town was only fifteen miles per hour. Brake lights flared, the driver's side door opened, and a leather covered foot landed on the pavement.

Khaki slacks came into view next as I stopped, waiting to see what this person would do. I wasn't too far away from them, but I was close enough to know that they had stopped for me.

Sandy blond disheveled hair obscured the man's face, until he looked up. His striking blue eyes connected with mine and I smiled, it was small, but noticeable to Eli.

"A little cold to be out for a stroll, huh?"

I nodded, "I'm not far from here. Perks of a small town."

He rubbed the smooth skin of his jaw with his hand, trying to cover his own answering smile. It was....cute. And damn if it didn't make me giggle. We were like awkward teenagers meeting up illicitly when our parents didn't know.

"Want a ride anyway?" He asked, hooking his thumb toward the rental he'd stepped out of.

I shook my head, biting the side of my lip to keep from smiling at how we'd both become bumbling idiots.

"Could you at least tell me where a guy can get a decent, greasy cheeseburger around here?"

My stomach grumbled on cue, reminding me that I hadn't eaten since my last snack before Bell left earlier.

He snickered, "I think your stomach likes that idea."

"More like the baby in it." I quipped. His eyes widened slightly, and I realized I'd said that louder than I meant to. Fuck me.

"Then let's feed that little monster, shall we?"

I would kill for a strawberry milkshake from Billy's, and Eli couldn't be a serial killer in disguise.

Could he?

If he killed me and stashed my body somewhere, I wouldn't be able to plan his brother's wedding. And he seemed pretty happy that we chose them from our applicants.

Looking both ways I headed for the passenger side of his rental and hopped in before I could change my mind.

Plus, Billy wouldn't let anything happen to me. He was closer to Bell, but he'd become a permanent fixture in my life too.

"I know the perfect place." I said, directing him to Billy's Chicken Pit.

Ronnie

Fifteen

Billy's Chicken Pit was a staple in this town, especially since Haven loved it and tweeted about it. He'd been swamped ever since, even over the holiday season. Although, he always closed the restaurant the week of Christmas.

It was my favorite time of the year, his too, I thought.

Eli parked in the gravel I directed him to. We usually parked near the back, just in case Billy let us eat in the kitchen. However, today I didn't think that would be the case with Eli in tow. Eli beat me to the door and opened it for me like a gentleman, complete with a bow.

"Charming." I snorted.

He smiled, eyes crinkling and teeth on full display. "So what makes this the best place to get a burger?"

I nodded to where Billy was sitting in a chair talking loudly with his grandson. Josh came into town for Christmas and hadn't left yet. I didn't know if he was planning to, since Billy was getting older and missed his family.

"That man, right there."

As if he'd heard me, Billy's head turned in our direction and I led Eli to a booth near the counter. His smile was contagious, and I was convinced he was the only person in the world no one could ever be mad at.

"Ronnie! Came for another milkshake?" He bellowed.

"Nah, Pop. Came to show this out of towner some good food."

"Well, I guess I can help y'all." His arms wrapped around my shoulders as he pulled me into a hug that smelled like grease and aftershave. A combination that should have made my pregnancy stomach sick, but no. Like I said, Billy could do no wrong.

"What'll you have, young man?" Billy said, handing only Eli a menu because he knew I didn't need one.

After giving it a quick look Eli said, "I'll take the fried chicken, okra, and corn."

"Ronnie?"

"I guess I will have that shake then." I sing-songed. "Oh! And some fries."

My stomach made an awful gurgling noise, and we all laughed. I loved the shakes because Billy refused to use syrup and vanilla ice cream base like most restaurants. He used actual strawberry ice cream blended up with local freshly grown strawberries and milk.

"Coming right up."

Eli turned to face me, eyes searching over me. His posture was laid back, as if he'd been here many times and fit in with the regulars. I had a feeling he was like that everywhere he went. His hair was still styled messily, curls falling onto his forehead.

"Thought you said you wanted a greasy burger?" I ribbed.

"Changed my mind." He inhaled like he wanted to continue but blew out his breath and shook his head instead.

Then he leaned in, like we were about to share a secret. "Can I ask you a personal, probably not my business, most definitely intrusive question?"

I laughed, actually snorted because that was a whole lot of words in one breath. "Sure." I said, waving my hand over the table.

"You're pregnant, but I don't see a ring."

"That was a question?"

He smiled and shook his head, curls bouncing from one corner of his head to the other. "It was, in a roundabout way." His eyes bounced over my face, as if he were watching my every facial muscle to determine if he'd just fucked up or not. "What I meant is, are you seeing anyone?"

My face flushed with heat, though I wasn't sure if he wanted to know because he was interested, or if he was simply curious because of the little bean in my uterus. *Fuck it.*

"No, I'm not seeing anyone."

He didn't say anything, just nodded and leaned back into the booth. I couldn't tell if he thought that news was good or bad. He gave nothing away. We both avoided each other's eye contact until Marcie came around with Eli's food.

"You should eat." I finally broke the weird silence, because he hadn't touched his food and I was fairly certain he was waiting for my milkshake to get to the table. His eyes lifted from where he's been staring and one side of his mouth lifted. "Wouldn't want Billy thinking his food isn't up to snuff."

"That would be rude." He agreed, slowly lifting his hand to where a spoon rested in the buttered corn.

"Plus, it's so much better when it's hot." I added, willing him to just take a damn bite of food.

He made a noncommittal noise in the back of his throat, but didn't lift the spoon. I sighed and reached across the table for a piece of his fried okra. Popping it into my mouth I tilted my head toward the plate.

Laughter erupted from him and he finally started in on his plate. He cut into the fried chicken with a fork and a knife. Which...okay. I'd only ever seen a few people do that here, and they weren't my favorite people.

"Extra cream," Billy said, sliding the pink goodness in front of me. "Just the way baby likes." He also came bearing extra crispy fries. That must have been why Eli got his food first.

"Thank you." I managed to get out before shoving a straw into the heavenly mixture and properly draining a quarter of it. I groaned and settled back into the old leather, bringing the milkshake with me.

Eli's spoon was resting half-way to his mouth, eyes wide, eyebrows skewed.

"Pregnancy craving," I said, raising both shoulders as I took another big gulp. He laughed, dropping his spoon back onto his plate and covering his stomach.

"Can't say I've ever seen a woman go absolutely feral over a milkshake before."

"I'm honored to be your first then." I bantered, shoving a few fries into my mouth.

He smiled, that lopsided grin and we continued to eat in silence. It was...nice. Having a meal with the opposite sex with no intentions of sleeping with them.

I finished my shake and wished like hell I could unbutton my pants, but thought better of it since this was my client's brother and all. Instead I settled for letting the old leather of the booth wrap around my body like a hug.

Watching him eat wasn't exactly what I planned on this evening, but it could've been worse. He was pretty to look at, and actually kind of funny in a laid back way. He didn't seem to be a serial killer, so really he had at least that going for him.

"Are *you* seeing anyone?" I blurted, my thoughts tending to tumble out unauthorized when I was thinking. It wasn't one of my finest qualities. He coughed a little, as if I caught him off guard. If he could ask, so could I.

"No, I don't really subscribe to the whole monogamy thing." He twirled his hand and pointed to his empty ring finger.

"Why not?"

He sighed, like he got that response a lot. But I *was* a wedding planner, I believed in true love. Just...not my own. What's left of my heart barely functioned now, I couldn't imagine tacking on someone else's.

"You don't have to answer that." I said after his long pause, because truly he didn't. He hadn't asked more about my situation, but I also didn't offer up details about it. Still, the way he looked back up at me now, it was a little crumb I couldn't help but latch on to.

"I don't mind," he started, "My parents didn't set the best example of husband and wife, lots of fights, cheating, debt. It all ended up becoming too much for either of them. Fights got too violent, voices were always too loud. So, the government decided we would be better cared for by Garret's grandmother." At my confused look he added,

"Garrett and I are half brothers on our mother's side. We moved in with her when we were fourteen."

"I'm sorry." Now I was the one who had asked a personal, probably not my business, most definitely intrusive question. "I shouldn't have asked."

"It's fine, honestly, Garrett and I," he wiped his mouth with a napkin and smiled, "We were better off with Grams."

Hearing the love and affection he carried for this woman who wasn't his grandmother made my already squirrely hormones go haywire. My eyes instantly watered, I couldn't get a napkin to the tears soon enough.

"Don't cry. Really, I've had a good life." He said, pushing napkins my way.

I wasn't crying for him, not totally. Hearing him talk about his family so openly had me thinking about mine. About how I could never be that open, even with a licensed therapist.

After I finished dabbing my eyes and blowing my nose Billy found us with a semi worried look. "Everything okay here?"

"Hormones." I sniffled.

I was sure Bell had told him a lot about my mood swings since my life kind of exploded. He just nodded and looked away, in the same direction he'd been looking with that wrinkled brow. I had to lean around Eli to see what he was looking at.

Or rather, who.

The moment I leaned over, dark eyes locked on mine and my entire body went rigid. Finn's body looked coiled, his face angrier than usual. Well, this just got really awkward.

"I think we'll take the check and head on." Flicking my eyes to Billy he nodded and hurried away to ring us up. I slid out of the booth as smooth as I could when Eli finally looked around, clueless.

"What are you running from, Ronnie?"

My name on his lips pulled me out of my fog. "What?"

His hand reached out for mine for a brief moment, "What's got you so spooked?"

Finn stood up from the table full of guys, and that's when I noticed Aaron was also there. He quickly found what had his best friend out of his seat and tried to pull him back. But Finn was a big man, and had already started our way when Eli said, "Isn't that the guy from earlier?"

I gulped. Full on, lots of spit down my throat, gulped. Twice now Finn had seen me with Eli, and if I was reading his face right, he looked pissed.

"Just roll with me. Whatever I say, nod." I whispered, hoping against all odds Eli heard me.

"Fancy meetin' you two here." Finn said, his deep timbre vibrating through my body. "Though, I recall your message said you were 'staying in' tonight."

Shit.

Wait.

"I didn't text you."

"You didn't have to Firecracker, we have mutual friends." He smirked and then I remembered why I was not currently friendly with him.

"Now you have my best friend's fiancé spying on me?" I yelled, loud enough I saw Aaron flinch. Good, rat. "You have no business doing that."

"Oh, but don't I?" He leaned against the booth, resting on one large forearm. "That baby in your body says otherwise."

I hated how blasée he was acting, how absolutely charming he could be, and I most definitely hated that my stupid, stupid lady brain had woken up at his mere proximity. But above all I hated that my brain stalled at the mention of my pregnancy.

"So, who's your friend here?" Finn spat the word 'friend' out like he'd been personally offended by the word.

"My *date*," I replied sweetly, "is Eli."

Eli didn't waste a minute, wrapping his hand around mine and pulling me closer. "Nice to meet you...." He said, offering Finn his other hand, waiting for someone to tell him Finn's name.

Something flickered across Finn's face as he grit out his name and shook Eli's hand way too forcefully to be anything civil.

"Nice to meet you, Finn. We were just on our way out, right Ronnie?"

"Yeah, my apartment isn't far from here." I looked up at him, hoping my little facade looked sultry.

Ronnie

Sixteen

The ride back to my house was silent. Because what do you say to the guy you just forced into a lie? Eli steered the car into a spot on the side of the street, maneuvering into a parallel spot easily.

He shut the engine off, but still didn't speak. We sat there, both unmoving, both silent. It was awkward and I caught myself holding my breath.

"Why are you running from him?" Eli's question jarred the silence in the car. Popping the bubble of denial.

"I'm not running from Finn." I scoffed and turned to face him. The street lights framed his golden hair in a halo through the tinted glass of the car. "What makes you think that?"

His brows furrowed before he shook his head and said, "Because the minute you saw him you wanted to leave. I'm still not even sure we paid that man back there, and you told him I was your date."

"Okay," I could see why he thought, maybe, I was scared of Finn. "We paid Billy, I have a tab...." I didn't know how to answer the last observation without shelling out all of my dirty laundry.

He kept eyeing me, like he knew it too.

I crossed my arms over my chest and waited. I could have a staring contest. I didn't need to do anything. Returning to my empty apartment to sit alone with my thoughts? No thank you.

"Why did you tell him I was your date, Ronnie?" Eli repeated.

I rolled my eyes and opened the door, the click of locks echoed over the near empty street. He'd tried to lock me in his car, the bastard. Who did he think he was?

"Ronnie." Eli said, his voice stern.

I turned to see him smoothly rising out of the car, keys firmly in hand making his way toward me. "You can't come up."

He smirked, "But I'm your date, isn't that what adults do after a successful date?"

"It wasn't a date." I said, stomping my foot down like a child. Eli was too damn cute, with his easy smirk and all seeing eyes. "We're friends."

"Are we?" he quipped, raising one eyebrow.

I nodded once, a short clip of my head.

"Because it seems to me like a friend would tell me why they are running from that man in the restaurant."

"Ugh," I threw my arms in the air, and walked to my building. Throwing the door open I glanced over my shoulder and said, "Are you coming in, or what?"

His long legs ate up the distance between the car and door, his smile on full blast as he gripped the door and motioned for me to enter. He followed me up the stairs to my apartment. When Bellamy moved out I downsized, I rarely stayed here anyways. I usually crashed at Bellamy's or Xavier's, hell even the shop sometimes.

I unlocked the door and went for the closet. Passing the couch, I told Eli to sit and promised to explain as much as I was willing to when I was finished changing. I might have groaned when I unbuttoned my pants.

I threw on a pair of navy leggings and exchanged my work shirt for a sweatshirt. I debated taking my bra off, but decided I could wait until after Eli left. Making my way back toward my living room I exhaled as my butt hit the soft cushions.

"I've known you for a handful of hours, and already, I'm your fictional date." Eli said, finally breaking the curtain of silence around us.

I inhaled and tried to arrange my thoughts. Eli wasn't my therapist, God knew I needed one, but he was sitting there, and apparently, willing to listen....

"Finn and I," I started, but it sounded all wrong, because there was no Finn and I. He'd made sure of that. I wracked my brain trying to come up with a way to continue. "We had a one night stand at the beginning of October. It was once, no names, just sex. The way I wanted it."

I ducked my head and stood up, crossing into the kitchen to retrieve water. Anything to relieve the pressure I felt from Eli's stare. I stood there, gulping water with my back turned on him.

"I never thought I'd see him again," I said after a while. "I thought, one and done. Just like the others..." It sounded bad when I said it out loud, but I wasn't ashamed of my sexual history. "It's one of my rules. One time, no strings, no repeats."

I slowly turned, forcing my eyes to find Eli's face, surprised to find a look of intrigue instead of displeasure. "Go on." He murmured and shook his hand.

"Except I couldn't get him out of my head. Then a few short weeks later, bam, pregnant. I knew it had to be his since I hadn't slept with anyone except him in months. It had been my longest drought period, ever."

I paused, drinking more water, then went pale because I hadn't even asked him if he wanted anything. I grabbed a bottle from the fridge and held it out for him, to which he shook his head and nodded for me to continue.

"A few days after I got a positive pregnancy test, I called him and we met up." This was officially the oddest conversation I'd ever had with a near stranger, but he was really easy to talk to. So I continued, "We decided to be friends, and raise this baby as co-parents. Naturally we began spending more time together since he was also my best friend's, now fiancé's, best friend. God has a wicked sense of humor, huh?" Laughing at myself as I drew in a deep breath ready to spill the hardest part of the story. "But the worst part isn't that they knew each other, it's that after we spent weeks getting closer than I ever have with a partner, Finn disappeared without a word."

"Right, and your best friend is Bellamy, your business partner, right?"

I nodded instead of speaking, because I was tired of talking. I didn't think I could share anymore without sending myself into a spiral. I also really needed to call Bellamy, because what Aaron did...not cool.

"Well, I'm in." Eli said with a throaty chuckle.

I whipped my head to look him square in the eyes. "What?" I think I said, because the way he was smiling looked like this was the most fun he'd had in a long time and he couldn't wait to fuck shit up.

He shrugged, "Why not? I'll have an excuse not to want to stab myself in the eye when we do all the inevitable wedding meetings, plus, you're stunning."

I didn't know if I should be flattered or offended.

"I'm not sleeping with you."

He threw his head back laughing, and raised his hands palms out, arms waving in x's. "I never thought you would." He said, subtly wiping the wetness from his eyes. "I actually made a promise to my brother that I wouldn't sleep with anyone while I'm here, and I think fucking the wedding planner would definitely cross that line."

I raised my brows because that was not what I was expecting him to say.

"So you, my fake girlfriend will be all the shield I need to not lose a thousand bucks."

Ronnie

Seventeen

After Eli left, I crashed into a deep sleep, not waking once. Being back in the office, after the renovations, was great, but tiresome. My brain pre-baby would have had me up all hours of the night, examining every word Eli and I exchanged, small blessings.

Sitting up in the bed I stretched my arms up, enjoying the cracking of my bones and stretching of my muscles. After I slid out from beneath the warm covers I set off into the small bathroom that afforded me everything I could need. The water was hot as I let it cascade down over my naked curves.

I'd had a hard time loving my body, not because I thought it was ugly, or less than, more feeling like it wasn't good enough, or broken somehow. Being told I may never be able to carry a baby was a blow. I didn't realize how much I wanted to eventually have kids until I was told I couldn't. The kicker was that it wasn't definitive testing. I was just told

I 'might' have trouble conceiving. Living with that hanging over my head, well, it sucked.

I held my hands over the little pooch of my stomach, and felt a few tears slip past my lashes. I was grateful for this little bean, but I couldn't help feeling like I'd already failed at giving him or her what I wanted too.

A family that stuck together no matter what. Something I didn't have.

My tears mingled with the water pouring out of the metal shower head. I didn't want to go back down that road, where the smell of smoke burned my nostrils and screaming rendered my mind useless.

I shook my head clear of those awful memories, and quickly showered. After I toweled off I searched for something to wear that didn't make me look like a hobo.

Throwing on a pair of leggings and a dress, I rifle through my shoes to find the most comfortable, yet stylish, ones I can find.

On my way out of the apartment I grabbed a banana and water. Breakfast of champions my friends.

Bellamy and I were meeting our clients at Thorns and Petals, the florist we used for all of our events. Misty was one of the loudest, most eccentric people we worked with, but she knew her flowers. What worked well together, what didn't. It's usually where Bellamy and I liked to start once we had our themes and colors worked out.

Since our clients hadn't been able to settle on anything we'd sent over, Bell and I decided to bring them into the flower shop for inspiration.

After the short walk to Thorns and Petals, I spotted Bell inside with Misty, already picking out flowers she thought would satisfy Stacey and Garrett.

Bell looked up and spotted me immediately though the window paned door. Her face broke out into a grin, but slowly morphed into a troubling scowl. Behind me I heard men's voices, but once they rounded the brick corner they stopped. Dark chocolate eyes fixed on mine and green ones darted around, looking anywhere but at me.

"Why are you here?" I blurted.

Our new couple wasn't famous, they didn't need protection. There was zero reason for Finn and Aaron to be here.

Aaron wiped his hand across the back of his neck, a clear sign of his discomfort. "I'm gonna," he pointed inside where I turned to find my best friend, arms crossed, scowling even deeper than she was a few minutes ago.

Aaron gave me a small smile as he went by, walking into the flower shop, and left Finn and I alone.

"Finally." Finn said by way of greeting. "I thought we'd never get another chance to talk."

I rolled my eyes, because the time for talking was when I called him four weeks ago, scared out of my mind that I was going to lose our baby.

He sighed, "Come on, Ronnie. Please don't shut me out forever."

I scoffed, "Try me."

His eyes lit up, I knew he had a sexual little quip queued up in that playboy brain of his and I didn't want to hear it. I raised my hand to stop him as he opened his mouth. "No sir, I do not want to hear it."

He smiled, and it lit his eyes up even more. It should have been a sin for him to look as good as he did. Standing there with his green Henley that covered his tattooed arms, stretched over corded muscles. The way his beard was perfectly trimmed and his hair was messily wavy in his signature half up half down bun.

It wasn't fucking fair!

"Can we please talk, somewhere without someone trying to light my ass on fire with their eyes?" Finn said, his deep voice almost pleading.

I turned my head over my shoulder to see Bell staring daggers at Finn. Reminding me that yes, he fucked up, but maybe...just maybe I could give him one more chance. I could hear him out. It would be nice to have unanswered questions answered so my brain would settle at night.

"Lunch," I offered.

"Whatever you want."

"Billy's, and you better show up. Not a minute later than noon, you hear me?" I tried to sound threatening, but it came off a little breathy because he was so stupid gorgeous. Hands in his pockets, rolling back on his heels and nodding like a kid who's been told to be good in order to get candy.

"And you better buy me a damn milkshake!" I shouted as we parted ways and Finn went wherever he'd been going with Aaron.

As he was walking away from me I grumbled under my breath, "don't make me regret this too…"

Finn

Eighteen

I was sitting in my truck when I saw Ronnie get out of the back of an Uber. Her shoulders tense and her usual smile gone. The gravel of the parking lot crunched under my feet as I got out to join her. In a few strides I was behind her gently touching her elbow so she knew it was me.

"Why didn't you tell me Bellamy or Aaron couldn't drop you off?"

"Because I'm not your problem, Finn."

Her blue eyes were full of steel, her face a mask of unreadable expression. I relented and looked away first, taking hold of the door I opened it and gestured for her to go inside. She did without any sassy remarks and immediately sat in the booth we always managed to sit in. Billy was nowhere to be seen, so he was probably in the kitchen cooking something up.

His grandson was back in town and when he saw us he smiled. The guy has grown on me, so I sent him a two finger salute and nodded to where Ronnie had just plopped down.

She didn't grab a menu because she knew it by heart, and with how often her and Bellamy ate here, I'd be worried if she didn't.

"Hi y'all!" Josh said when he got close enough to the table. "Pop's in the back if you need him."

"Hey, man. First things first, I need a strawberry milkshake 'Ronnie style'." I could practically hear her glower, so I threw her a wink.

We ordered, and I got whatever the special today was while Ronnie decided on chicken fingers and fries with the strawberry milkshake I'd ordered for her. She leaned back in the booth, expectant eyes finally meeting mine.

"I'm sorry for being-"

"A dick? A sorry sack of shit?" Ronnie jumped in and supplied.

I looked away from her for a second and took a deep breath. "Absent." I said, making sure to look at her once again. Her mouth popped open as if she didn't expect me to admit it. "I should have been there, and instead I fell into my own head."

She nodded, seeming to consider my words.

"I struggled with it, I know I'm not the ideal person you want to raise a baby with. Then I started researching, I wanted to know everything I could about raising a baby. I wanted to be prepared. I wanted to be the person you would want to raise this child with." I watched her face as I admitted all of the things I was scared of at first. Her lips turned down into a frown and her eyes melted, as if she's going to cry.

"I'm sorry, Ronnie. I know that doesn't make up for the missed appointments or all the weeks I disappeared on you."

She shook her head, shoulders hunched in toward her body. She started to speak, but nothing came out, as if she didn't know the words she wanted to use.

"Did I make you feel that way?" She finally said, eyes holding so much emotion it was hard for me to not want to touch her. To offer her some sort of anchor in this moment.

"No." I answered honestly, because it wasn't her, it was my own fear.

"Why now?"

"Because I have really good parents who helped me on my journey to becoming the man I want to be for us." I couldn't help the laugh that bubbled out of my chest. "That and Aaron flew down to kick my ass." My parents would love Ronnie, especially since she asked if she was the cause of my breakdown. Her heart was one of the reasons I lo– wanted this life with her.

Aaron really did kick my ass though, being as close to Ronnie as he was, he noticed her lack of a partner, and knew I'd end up back here with her.

"Us." She said, not a question but a statement.

I nodded, because even though I knew I would have come around eventually on my own, the damage would have been that much worse.

"Why couldn't you just talk to me?" Her voice cracked and her eyes beseeched me.

"I don't know why, I wish I did. I spent so much time reading every book I could, going to classes, trying to figure out how I could be an equal partner for you. Someone you'd be proud to raise a child with."

I was laying out all of my cards, because even though I knew Ronnie better than I had, I didn't know her fully. I didn't know her story, or why she'd guarded her heart for so long, but I wanted to. I wanted to know everything about the beautiful woman across from me.

The woman who'd stolen my heart right from my chest in a dark hallway one random night.

Josh came back with Ronnie's shake, breaking the tense conversation. Ronnie's eyes grew large as she spotted the milkshake Josh made. It was piled high with whipped cream, and strawberries dotted the rim.

Her glee was contagious and I smiled at her. He promised our food would be right out and left Ronnie slurping up a dollop of fluffy white sugar.

"I will do whatever it takes to prove I'm here, Firecracker." I told her while she licked her pink lips. "And that I'm never going anywhere again."

After a long drag from her straw she said, "Okay." She sank her teeth into her bottom lip, "But it's strictly platonic. I can't let myself get attached to you again, at least in *that* way."

I nodded, knowing that if that's all I could get, I'd take it. For now.

Ronnie

Nineteen

It had been a whirlwind the past few weeks. Between dress shopping for Stacey, planning her wedding, handling Finn's attitude about my fake boyfriend Eli, and doctor's appointments, I'd hardly had a moment to myself. Finn had been hounding me for a while wanting to go to an ultrasound, and complaining that the pictures I'd sent him weren't "sufficient".

I caved and that's how I found myself sitting in his big truck, arms tucked into my body. I didn't *want* to want Finn, but my body sure did. Every time he was around, my body got hot and my mind couldn't concentrate on anything other than him.

The tattoos that ran up and down his arms were my catnip, and even though he'd been wearing long sleeves I still remembered them. The harsh lines of black ink and swirls of color mixing together to create the beautiful art on his body. With his messy hair and dark beard that lined his jaw, I couldn't keep my eyes away from him.

Ever since I told Finn I couldn't be intimate with him again it's like my body was trying to revolt. In my head I knew why I set that boundary, but my libido apparently didn't get that memo.

I sighed, leaning my head on the cool glass.

"That was a heavy sigh."

Damn it.

"Just nervous." I lied.

The side of his mouth tipped up in a smirk that I'd become so used to seeing, and my stupid vagina started to tingle. He shouldn't be able to be this attractive. It should be outlawed.

He adjusted his grip on the steering wheel, the rose there flexed, and the numbers on his knuckles disappeared. He placed a gentle hand on my thigh to keep my leg from bouncing.

I almost purred like a cat in heaven, because it had been a while. Too long without physical affection from a living breathing person. Not that my battery operated boyfriend wasn't getting the job done...it was just different.

We pulled into the doula's office parking lot and I eyed Finn. I didn't recall telling him where the appointment was.

His cheeks reddened slightly, "I looked it up after Aaron let it slip."

I nodded, because what else could I do? We ran in the same circles now, and it was sometimes...nice. He unlocked the doors and we climbed out. He was already striding around the cab when my foot landed on the pavement.

His hand navigated the small of my back, pushing me slightly so he could shut the door. The heat from his palm was warm and comforting. I took a few deep breaths as we headed for the front door.

Regina looked up from whatever she had been busy doing and gave me a big smile that I returned. Getting to know these two had been the best experience. Her eyes widened slightly when Finn walked through the door, then immediately narrowed, and I started to worry.

"This him?" She nodded to indicate Finn lurking behind me, and if I didn't love her already, I would when she followed it up with, "About damn time you showed up."

She didn't shout, and Finn just stood there, his hand still on my lower back. "I guess you've heard of me."

"Oh boy, have I?" She laughed, but there wasn't any humor behind it. I shifted so I could watch her give him absolute shit for dodging me. "This angel here has had to do everything alone, and now you want to show up?"

"Ma'am..." He started but Regina was not having it. She rounded her desk and stepped up to Finn like my own personal avenging angel.

"Don't 'ma'am' me! Veronica is one of the strongest people I know, and I've watched a woman push out a ten pound baby with no drugs." Her finger punctuated every word as she jabbed it into his chest. "Now, if it were me, and thank your lucky stars it's not, I would have cut your manhood straight off your body and fed it to the koi in our next door neighbor's office."

I saw him gulp and decided to save him, for now.

"Regina," I giggled, "I think he gets it."

She turned and flounced back to the desk and I had the distinct feeling that her and Bellamy would be fast friends provided the chance.

"You're all set Veronica." She said as she typed furiously on her keyboard. "And please do let me know if you need any assistance, anything at all."

I couldn't help the explosive laugh that burst from my chest when Finn quickly followed me to the room Regina told me to go to.

Finn

Twenty

The room Ronnie closed us into was impressive. A television sat on the far wall in front of the chair beside the table she was climbing onto. Everything was painted in neutral colors and pictures lined the walls.

I sat in the chair against the wall, slowly taking everything in. Ronnie started to lift her dress up and I immediately jumped up to cover her with my body. Even though there was no one in here there could be cameras. Right?

"Uh, Finn." She said, clutching her dress and staring at me like I'd lost my damn mind. "What are you doing?" I mumbled, trying to readjust her dress, not so subtly looking around for onlookers.

She laughed and my thoughts jumbled. "The doctor has to put the machine over my uterus to see our baby."

The way she said our baby made my stomach flip. There wasn't any animosity, nothing to suggest she was upset, and she didn't seem resigned or regretful. I could almost imagine she seemed genuinely...happy.

"What?" she said, and I realized I'd just been staring at her for the better part of the past five minutes.

"You said our baby."

"Well it is our baby." Her eyes bounced between mine, brows furrowed. "Are you okay? I know Regina can be..."

"I'm great." I interrupt because I do not want to think about that woman and her threat. The expression on her face was filled with mirth and she finished getting settled, tucking a blue sheet of paper into her panties.

"What's the napkin for?" I asked. genuinely curious.

Ronnie laughed and it was light and melodic, "So the gel doesn't get on my undies."

"Oh."

I couldn't think of anything else to say, so we sat there, in comfortable silence and it hit me that I was about to see the little human we made together. I didn't know what to expect and I started to get a bit nervous that I might embarrass her.

There was a knock on the door and when Ronnie answered with a shouted "come in", a woman with deep copper skin, dressed in a yellow dress swept into the room. Her eyes lit up when she looked at Ronnie and when they focused on me she offered her hand.

"I'm doctor Ashton Steele." Her hands were strong and I didn't know why that surprised me.

"Finn Hart." I offered, even though I was pretty sure she knew who I was.

"It's very nice to meet you, Finn. I've heard a lot about you."

She embraced Ronnie in a quick hug and set up the machine on the other side of her. She squeezed a clear, jelly-like substance all over Ronnie's exposed skin and I tried not to look as confused as I felt.

"We're going to go ahead and do the anatomy scan today. It's a little early, but with your condition I don't want to wait."

My mind got stuck on the 'condition' part of her statement. What condition was Ronnie in? Or was it the baby? Why hadn't we talked about this?

Ronnie's hand slipped out to grip mine, effectively pulling my mind from the racing questions. "Can we skip the gender?"

"Why?" I said at the same time the doctor said, "Of course."

"I want it to be a surprise." She whispered, her hand gently squeezing mine. I didn't say anything, thinking instead about having a boy or a girl. The lists that started in my head began to fill.

The sound was unlike anything I had ever heard. Like I was underwater, ears filled with hushed sounds, listening to the propeller of a boat chopping at water. It was difficult to describe, but I found it soothing to my ears.

It was an odd sound, but unmistakably the baby's rapid heartbeat. I'd heard it a thousand times watching as many YouTube videos on birth as I could. Tears pricked behind my eyes, and I swiped them with my thumb and forefinger before looking at the monitor.

The grainy image reflected our baby, the curve of its little nose, how it moved as if suspended in time, it didn't seem real.

Dr. Ashton was rattling off the things they checked during the scan while the machine started to print out screenshots of the ultrasound. I couldn't see much else because my eyes hadn't been able to leave the television screen showcasing the growing being inside of Ronnie.

My chest squeezed and my lungs felt too big for my body all at once. It hit me again, I'm going to be a father, but I didn't think I'd feel this. This... fear and anxiety swirling inside me. I had no doubt it was because of the baby on the screen.

I felt like my body could burst with all the emotions clogging my veins. I swiveled my face to Ronnie's, she's watching the screen too. Eyes glued to the little black and white being in her body.

"I'm going to do a quick scan of the anatomy, so if you don't want to be spoiled I can turn the screen off." Dr. Steele said.

Ronnie nodded and flexed her hand in mine. The screen went black and I eagerly awaited the doctor's words.

"Looks like you two will have a healthy baby. Ronnie, keep doing what you're doing. Low activity, eat every couple of hours, and lots of rest."

"I will." Ronnie assured her.

After they exchanged a few more words the doctor left and Ronnie used the tissues the doctor left and cleaned up the clear jelly liquid off her little bump.

We didn't speak as we made our way back to the truck. I didn't trust myself to have the right words after that. I had questions, a lot of them actually.

"What did the doctor mean, when she said 'in your condition'?" I couldn't hold my tongue any longer. I needed to know that she was okay.

"Caught that, huh?" She sighed, "I have a bicornuate uterus."

"A bi-what?"

She laughed a little at my confusion. "It's a double-sided uterus, basically a heart where it should be just a hollow 'U' shaped."

"I don't understand." I admitted, because what did it matter what her uterus looked like?

"It's rare, and most women who have it have trouble getting pregnant, but if by some miracle they get pregnant, they have a higher chance of miscarrying." I watched her shrug out of the corner of my eye.

"How will that affect you and the baby?" I was so curious, I didn't know anything about this. But I was going to do every bit of research I could on the matter.

"As long as I continue to do what I've been doing, I think both of us will be okay."

"Is there anything I can do to make it easier?" I wanted to fix all of her problems, but this wasn't one I could tackle on my own.

She twisted her body toward mine and smiled, "Just show up."

I drove us back to her tiny apartment in silence once more. I knew she wasn't trying to hurt me by reminding me to show up, but my thoughts were working overdrive to think of all the things I needed to research and understand.

When I pulled up to the door she hopped out before I could stop her.

"I'll let you know if there are any updates." She said laying the envelope of sonograms on the seat.

Aaron called as I backed the truck out of my spot in front of Ronnie's place.

"Hey, man!" His cheery voice boomed over the speakers. "How'd it go?"

"It was...I-I don't even know man. Unreal." Words failed me again. There were so many I could use to describe it, too many words, wild, surreal, unbelievable. In the same breath, there weren't nearly enough.

"I can't imagine." He said.

We sat in silence for a moment, that was our friendship. We enjoyed the silence together, no need to fill the peace with needless words.

"I have a favor to ask." Aaron broke the silence, his tenor was serious.

"Sure."

"Meet me at the address I just texted you?"

I agreed and plugged in the address to my phone. Following the winding back streets of our small town I spotted Aaron standing beside his truck, shoulders pressed back looking at three houses sitting side by side. All with for sale signs in their yards.

I pulled into the drive where he had parked and got out. "You and Bellamy thinking about buying a house?"

He turned to face me, cheeks a little pink from the cold and nodded. "Follow me."

Trailing behind him up the drive he practically vibrated with energy. He took the small steps two at a time, booted feet stomping the freshly stained wood.

He plugged a code into the lock box around the door handle and out fell a key. Unlocking the door he waved me in. The place was empty, which made sense for a new build. I could still smell the paint drying on the walls and the sweet smell of cut lumber.

The kitchen was to the right, a big island topped in black and white marble dominated the space. Olive green cabinets lined the walls, and black matte appliances sat in their places with yellow stickers still attached.

"It's bigger than what we originally planned on." Aaron started, "but I figure we'll grow into it."

I nodded, still eyeing the space. The living room was to the left, a stone fireplace sat in the corner. Stairs split the two rooms straight in front of the door we walked through. It didn't, however, interrupt the flow of the house.

"And there's the house next door..."

I whipped my head sideways to stare at him. Was he...asking me to buy the house next door?

"I figured, with the baby coming, y'all might want some close hands. You know, for help."

I laughed then, "You think Ronnie will move in with me?"

He rubbed the back of his neck and sighed. "The things I do for her." He smiled a bit more before clearing his throat and continuing. "The arrangement was Bellamy's idea."

Surprise lit up my insides. I knew Bellamy and I didn't really see eye to eye on a lot of things, but maybe she was seeing the effort I'd been putting in.

"So she would help convince Ronnie to move in with me?"

Hope flared in my chest, we could really make this work. The three of us on the same page, Ronnie couldn't possibly have too many objections.

I needed to have a chat with Bellemy and get her on my side.

Ronnie

Twenty-One

"You did what?" I screeched at my best friend.

Bell just told me her and Aaron bought a house and a car, considering she won't be able to walk to work anymore with the location of the property. Buying a house shouldn't surprise me. They had moved fast when they met, so why should buying a place of their own together shock me?

Maybe because she's moving on, and I'm still stuck in this in-between? I don't know where I want my life to go. What I do know, is that logically I can't stay in my studio apartment, it's not the ideal location for a baby to grow up.

"I can't wait for you to see it." She gushed, her cheeks rosy.

"Are you selling your old place?" I asked, it was a great location, and it could be mine. Alone.

She eyed me curiously, "Yeah."

"Maybe I could buy it from you?" I said kind of in a question statement twist. Clearing my throat I tried again. "I mean, it's a perfect size for me and the baby, and you know I've always loved your place. Win, win!"

Bell wouldn't look at me, instead she rearranged her desk. Slamming things down in the exact place it was before.

"Bellamy-soon-to-be-Lark. What is the matter with you?" I stood and placed my hand on hers before she could slam down her drink for a third time.

"I can't." She whispered. I'd never heard her sound so little before.

"I know it needs some work, but it would be the perfect spot for me to raise my little bean."

It would too, a cute little house with a white picket fence to keep my little rascal from running out of the yard. The close quarters. Some paint and a little more decor, it could be *home*.

"It needs more than some work, Ronnie." She flicked her eyes over my face, which had no doubt fallen from her lack of enthusiasm. "I won't sell it to you."

"Why not?"

My temper was starting to get the best of me, and Eli was coming soon to take me out on our first official fake date. The last thing I wanted was to have him think twice about our arrangement because I was fighting with my best friend over a house.

Bellamy sighed and reclined in her chair. "I just think maybe you should talk to the Behemoth before you decide to buy a house for you and your child."

I cut my eyes at her. How dare she play him like a card in Uno. I was about to plus four this bitch.

"The same man who disappeared for weeks without a fucking word, before finally deciding he wanted to take part in raising *our* child?" Her face fell and it hit me. She was concocting a plan, they all were conspiring behind my back. "What do you have up your sleeve, Bellamy?"

"For the record, you were not supposed to find out this way." Her cheeks flushed as she looked over my shoulder, then back to me. "And you have to know this is not how I wanted it to happen."

Aaron was in the doorway when I turned around, and a suspiciously Finn shaped shadow was moving back down the hallway.

"You ambushed me?" I said, twirling around to eye my supposed best friend.

"I know Finn hurt you, and I don't forgive him....yet." She added when Aaron cleared his throat. "Doesn't everyone deserve a second chance, Tink?"

How dare she use my nickname. I couldn't process my feelings. It felt like everyone was against me, even though I had been willing to give Finn another chance, it had to be on *my* terms, not anyone else's.

"I hate that you're all bulldozing me into resolving my shit with Finn, and I hate that you may be right. Even if that's true, Bell, you're supposed to be in *my* corner." I couldn't control the cracks in my voice, or the tears from welling in my eyes. "I've got to go."

"Ronnie." Aaron started, but I pushed past him and started for the door.

Eli was reaching for the handle when I pulled it open and pushed past him, looking for Finn. He stepped back, but didn't say anything.

I looked back and forth, across the street, even took a few steps to view around the corner, but he was gone. I shouldn't feel bad for having the feelings that I did, I know I'm allowed to feel betrayed, and lied to. I also know Bellamy just wants me loved and taken care of, and she wants to make sure Finn is stepping up. I guess he is trying, which I appreciated, but I was tired of everyone forcing my hand. I needed to be able to forgive Finn when I was good and ready.

"Baby daddy went that way." Eli said, sticking his thumb up over his shoulder. "Do we need to reschedule?"

I leveled him with a glare. "No."

His hands went up, palms facing me. "Okay."

He nodded to where his car was parked on the side of the street and we walked over together. Helping me in, he waited until I was buckled before closing the door and walking around to his side.

We didn't speak as he drove us into Charleston. The text he sent me told me to wear something nice, but not too fancy. After practically cleaning out my closet I settled on yellow flare pants that I found while scourging an online yard sale for pregnancy clothes. They were bright and cheery, two of my favorite things.

A white blouse that bunched around my breasts to show off my bump, with sheer billowing sleeves finished off the ensemble. The shirt had crochet over the bust in floral patterns that made me giddy every time I looked down. It was subtle, but feminine in a way I loved.

I still wore my tan chunky heels. My feet would be killing me if we did much walking, but I couldn't fathom not wearing them with the outfit. I paired it with the gold pendant Bellamy gave me all those years ago after our very first heart-to-heart.

It's rare that I ever take this particular necklace off at all.

Gold hoop earrings dangle daintily from my ears, and I did my makeup like I do every day. Standard concealer for the sleepless nights that left me with bruised looking under eyes. Foundation to cover the freckles that dotted my face. A swipe of liner across my lids and a peachy nude for my lips.

Hit the lashes with a little mascara, and viola!

If this pregnancy was the only one I got to have, I was going to do it in style. Dr. Steele hadn't specifically told me this little one would be it for me, but I'd done my research, and this miracle shouldn't have been possible.

Eli pulled the car smoothly in front of a busy looking restaurant. The awning was dark blue, with glass covering the front. Inside it looked like a fun pub, all dark wooden paneled walls, industrial lighting lined the ceiling, emitting a warm yellow glow.

The tables were covered in white linens and a little vase with a candle sat in the middle of each one. It felt like a real date, and I guess my face showed my hesitation when Eli placed a hand on my back to guide me behind the hostess.

He leaned down so he could speak in my ear. "It's not as fancy as you think."

I eye'd the place again, settling on his smiling face. "I can see we have a different opinion on 'fancy.'"

When we got to our table he pulled my chair out for me before rounding the table to sit down himself.

The perfect gentleman.

The waiter came over with two waters filled with ice and a lemon slice on the side. He asked if we'd like to know the daily special and if we wanted to order any other drinks.

Eli ordered an old fashioned, and I asked for a black cherry soda.

"Should I be worried about you drinking and driving a pregnant lady around?" I teased, knowing most likely if he got any buzz it would be long gone by the time we got done with dinner.

"No," he smirked, "but you probably should worry about the big brute who followed us here."

I whipped around, spotting Finn with his arm hanging out of his truck window, staring at us through the clear windows.

"I can't believe him!" I said, throwing my napkin down and making to stand.

Eli's hand shot out, grabbing mine before I could get up. "Just let him stalk."

"I'm mad at him though, and I really need a good yell."

I watched Eli's smirk increase to a full-blown smile.

"Honestly, I think I'm holding up my side of the bargain nicely." He chuckled and I couldn't help but laugh too. My hair brushed the small of my back as I tipped my head back, the longest it's been in a while.

"Crushing the fake dating game." I exclaimed.

The waiter returned and took our order, placing a bread basket beside the vase candle, and I slathered a big hunk of butter on a piece and stuffed my face. It was soft and buttery goodness. Carbs were my favorite. Which I think is what made Bellamy and I fall in love with each other.

Thinking of her made my chest ache. I shouldn't have been so upset. I didn't even know what they had conspired about without me, but I was sick of it all the same.

"Graham said Stacey is loving the way everything is going for the wedding so far." Eli began. This was how our conversations normally went. Neutral zone topics, but to anyone inspecting from the outside we looked like a comfortable couple.

I guess in a way, we were. Eli was safe. I knew where I stood with him, and I knew I could stand without him if I needed to. I didn't love him, nor did I think we were anything but friends who would part once his brother married.

Outlining the terms made me feel less attached, peaceful in our mutual decision. We could be friends without me having to worry that he was leaving and that he wasn't going to change his mind.

Losing people was one thing I didn't do well. So knowing our 'relationship' had an expiration date helped me. There would be no spiral when he left, just fond memories of our time together.

We ate, laughed, all while Finn stayed parked across the street. I could hear the loud rumble of his truck pulling off and circling the block to come back, obnoxious boys and their toys. Eli confirmed when he had to cover his laugh with a hand.

The food was good, nowhere near as good as Billy's, but it would suffice. I really wanted a milkshake, and when Eli asked, the waiter looked at him funny and came back with the news that they did in fact use syrup in vanilla ice cream to make their chocolate milkshake.

No strawberries in sight.....that should be a crime.

Eli paid the bill and we walked out to where he parked the car. As we did, Eli made sure to slip his hand into mine, twisting our fingers together. I could almost envision Finn's teeth mashing together.

Could practically hear it.

I had to stifle a laugh when Eli brushed a kiss over my cheek before closing my door. No doubt he was smirking at Finn, who had started his truck and slowly drove by.

"I almost feel bad for the guy," Eli shared with me on the way back to my apartment.

I laughed then. "Don't. This is harmless, I could do worse."

"You devious little creature!" Eli said, his voice like a scandalized socialite. We laughed and chatted until he dropped me off and I spotted Finn leaned up against the brick beside the door to my apartment.

Well, this was going to be fun.

Ronnie

Twenty-Two

His feet were crossed at the ankles, his long sleeve shirt bunched around his impressive muscles. It wasn't fair how attractive he was. The worst part of it all was he didn't flaunt it. He knew he looked good, but he remained humble about his figure.

"Are we adding stalker to our resume tonight?" I asked, keeping my face neutral.

"I wouldn't have to stalk you if you'd just talk to me." His deep voice carried over the cold air between us, and I shivered. He nodded his head toward the door. I sighed but allowed him to follow me up to my apartment.

It was messy, as per usual, I didn't have enough storage for clothes. My kitchen had approximately three usable cabinets, and next to no counter space. Billy installed some shelves for me on one wall for linens, not that I had use for much of them, being alone and all.

"You're the one who ran away." I stated. It was a low comment, since he only ran because I was losing my shit on Bellamy.

"What would you have done in my shoes, Ronnie?" He plopped down on my sofa and ran his hand over his face. "I'm trying."

I nodded and turned on my chunky heel, heading for the small bathroom tucked beside my closet. Unbuttoning my pants I let out a little sigh of relief. Okay, a huge sigh of relief.

Wiggling the material over my butt and thighs I stepped out of the bright yellow pants, and pulled off my blouse. Standing here looking at my reflection wearing nothing but a bra, panties, and my chunky heels I felt powerful.

My belly had rounded out a lot in the past weeks, like my bean finally said, "I'm here, mommy!"

Tears stung the back of my eyes as I took the time to twist and observe my body from all angles. My boobs were already a nice size, but they had gotten bigger, filling out my bras a little more.

I felt...beautiful and strong.

"Are you avoiding me in your bathroom?" Finn's voice broke the trance I found myself in, and I couldn't help the little cough-laugh that slipped out.

"No." I choked out, my throat still thick from allowing myself the space to feel.

Slipping on some leggings and a long t-shirt I swept my hair up into a messy bun on the top of my head. Grabbing water from the fridge I sat beside Finn, pulling my legs up under me so I sat crisscrossed, body angled toward him.

He looked me over, his eyes lingering on the bump of my stomach. "I don't really know how to be..." he took a deep breath, as if whatever thoughts he had churning through his brain left him vulnerable. "I want to be a partner to you, Firecracker. I want to be the person you call when you're sad, stressed, hormonal. I want to be there, for you, and for our baby."

I didn't know what to say. I'd wanted to hear those words for a long time, every doctor's appointment he missed, every time I cried for no reason. It took him a while, and I understand a little why he was absent, but I still didn't completely trust his words. His actions were more convincing to me lately, and I found myself softening more and more.

"I promise, I'm all in." He said, dipping his head down so he could meet my eyes.

"We need some boundaries," I said, maybe not the brightest while he's being so sincere. "I appreciate your honesty, it's going to take me some time to rebuild that trust with you, but I'm willing to try. And no more using Aaron and Bellamy as mediators, that was shitty and you know it."

Finn nodded, his lips tipping up in a devastating smile, "Deal."

"But, before we move on from Bell. Tell me why she was so adamant that I should talk to you before I make living arrangements."

"We don't have to talk about that right now," Finn quickly said.

"Finn," I admonished.

He leaned back, eyes wide, looking everywhere but at me. "I..."

"You bought a house, didn't you?" I said, finally putting all the pieces together like a puzzle.

He had the good sense to look a little ashamed. "It's next door to Aaron and Bellamy. The perfect place to start a family."

"But..."

"I know," he cut me off, "you don't want to make anything complicated. But in everything I've read, it says that raising a baby takes a village. I didn't think when I saw the house, I just impulse bought, but I understand if you don't want..."

I laid my hand on his arm, stopping him from his word vomit, "I'd like to see it."

He didn't expect that, and I had to duck my head to hide my smile.

"Really?" He sounded cautious, and I couldn't blame him. So, I smiled and nodded at him.

We sat in silence for a while, unspoken words floating around the air. We still had a lot more to work out, but right now, I felt content. We watched a movie and Finn rubbed my feet until the credits rolled and I was almost asleep.

"Come on." He said, sliding one arm under my knees and the other behind my back. "Let's get baby to bed."

I laughed and allowed him to carry me the short distance to my bed, where he gently placed me in the middle and covered my body with the many blankets I'd eventually shed off in the middle of the night.

He started for the door, "Finn?"

"Firecracker?" He mocked me.

"I'm glad you're trying."

"Meet me at Billy's tomorrow after work," Finn said before walking out with a proud puff of his chest.

Finn

Twenty-Three

After last night with Ronnie, I left feeling like we could actually make this work. It would take more than one good night, but we'd both agreed to try. I wanted to show her a little about my world, my why.

She knew I liked to work out, and I did, I just wanted to show her it's not all weights and 'bro' back slaps every time you finish a set.

"I signed us up for couples yoga," I told her around a bite of my burger. Billy's had been a staple in Ronnie's new diet. I watched her devour the milkshake she had become obsessed with recently, strawberries and cream.

Ronnie couldn't get enough of the stuff.

I didn't say anything about all the sugar she'd been ingesting, because my poor Firecracker hadn't been able to keep much in her stomach.

Her doula told us that every pregnancy was different. Some have pregnancy sickness through all forty weeks, some don't get sick at all. It's really dependent on the person.

I felt bad enough for missing so much of the first trimester, I couldn't deprive her of her sugar now.

"For what reason, Behemoth?" She said, lapping up the extra whipped cream Billy piled on for her.

"It's healthy for mom and baby to move." I told her, proud of all the parenting books I had read, and maybe, slightly, trying to gain common ground. "Plus, Dr. Steele told us to make sure you kept up healthy habits."

"You really need to stay off those parentings sites." She leaned back, and looked around. "And I distinctly remember her saying to *rest*."

I smiled, watching her as she tried to discreetly unbutton her jeans without moving her shirt. She fussed with it for a few more minutes before giving in and lifting her shirt. The jeans she had on were already for pregnant women, with the stretchy mesh. She didn't care though, because anytime she'd eaten anything that made her stomach full, and her heart happy, the buttons came undone. It was one of her quirks that never failed to make me smile.

"I read that in a book."

"You can read?" She said, laying her hand over her heart.

"Ha-Ha, Firecracker." I joked, "I did graduate high school somehow."

She smirked at me while rubbing her bump. "Of course you did, *daddy*."

My dick twitched in my sweatpants at the nickname. Goddamn, this woman. Her smirk was devious, like she knew exactly what she was doing.

I leaned forward, close enough to her side of the table to whisper, "Keep it up and I'll never wear anything but gray sweat pants again, see how *'platonic'* this can really be."

Her smirk faded away, morphing into a frown. I'd hit a nerve. This was something we hadn't talked about since our agreement to stay out of each other's pants, and I had a feeling that she was reminiscing about the last outcome of us having sex.

I knew we both had our fun, and I wasn't judging her for it, especially since I was whoring it up until a few months ago when I got her call.

It changed my whole perspective, I wasn't proud of the way I handled my end of the situation for the first few weeks. I'd hurt her, unintentionally. While cleaning up my life, I went radio silent. I was starting to understand that abandonment was triggering for her.

I didn't know all of the trauma life had thrown at her. I wanted to though, I wanted to know everything about her. Ever since our illicit night against that wall in a dark hallway in my sisters club, I think my heart knew she would walk away with it, and never give it back.

The way her eyes melted, back arched, breaths harsh and whispered, I knew, and I didn't fucking care. What did I need with the stupid organ anyway?

What I didn't expect was for her to steamroll in alongside my best friend Aaron. Bellamy was cool, gruff, and she loved Ronnie like no one else. It was an adjustment realizing I had all these other people to share my Firecracker with even before I got to have her all to myself.

I wanted nothing more than to love Ronnie like a man dying and she was the only drug that could save me.

I just needed to find a way to start doing it, without her getting spooked.

Her frown stayed turned down as she finished off her shake. I watched her spoon out the remainder of the melted whipped cream she loved and smile, trying to lighten the mood. "I was only joking. I know you don't want a relationship, even though you're still hanging out with 'surfer dude.'"

"Hanging out sounds so juvenil." She said, scrunching her nose. "We're friends."

"That's what you're calling it?" I smirked, knowing full well she wasn't doing anything remotely close to intimate with Eli.

She made her signature *mmmmmhmmmm* as she slurped up the bottom of the milkshake. Her lips wrapped around the straw, and my threat from a second ago had me readjusting myself as discreetly as I could.

Her eyebrow cocked upward, and her lips lifted into a coy smile. She knew what she was doing, and it only confused me more, because Ronnie was who she was, seductive, playful, and funny. It would be hard for any man not to fall for her.

"So couples yoga, huh?" She said as she leaned back in her chair to let the milkshake settle.

I smiled, "Tomorrow at 7am!"

She grumbled, like I knew she would, but nodded.

The next morning I picked her up from her apartment that I hated. She was flinging clothes across the room from where her makeshift closet stood. Shirts and pants flew across the air landing somewhere on the floor or couch she had positioned perfectly on the light hardwoods.

I thought again about her reaction to me buying the house next door to Aaron and Bellamy. The hurt and anger in her voice when Aaron and I came to surprise her. It stung more than it should have.

"What does a pregnant girl wear to couples yoga anyway?" Ronnie all but screamed into her ceiling.

I laughed into my hand, because I sure as hell didn't want her to sit and refuse to come. "Just wear something comfortable."

"I'm pregnant, Finn. Nothing is comfortable."

"I'll massage your feet again if you just throw something on." I wasn't above the bribe, plus I loved touching her. Any excuse to do it, and I was there.

She poked her head around the screen she used for privacy and said, "Really?"

I chuckled, "Really, now get your ass in gear!"

Playful Ronnie was my favorite version. Her spunky attitude and verbal sparring were everything I didn't know I needed. She wore black leggings that went over her bump and a bright orange top that hung off her shoulder slightly.

"What shoes do I wear?" She asked, her eyes roaming over her collection.

"Something you can take off easily."

She bent down, shuffled through more shoes than one person needed and pulled out a pair of flip flops. Throwing them down on the floor she slid them over her feet and declared that she was ready to go.

The drive to the gym was quiet, except for Ronnie moving constantly in the passenger seat.

"Nervous?" I asked, slightly amused.

Her eyes slid my way, but she didn't respond. I let it go, unwilling to push her too far. I parked the truck in my usual spot. They weren't assigned, I just always tended to park in the same place.

We hopped out of the truck, and I led her through the front doors of my safe haven, Wadey Weights. It immediately felt like bricks being lifted off my shoulders. Plus having Ronnie here, it felt like coming home.

"Hi Finn!" Jenny said as I scanned my card in. "Gotta friend today?"

Jenny was the owner's daughter, so I'd known her for a while. Since she was a gangly thirteen year old who thought all her problems could be solved with boys. She was around twenty something now, with long dark hair that's always in a ponytail.

"Yeah, this is Ronnie." I said, gesturing to the woman of my dreams next to me.

"Oh! You're *her*!" Jenny squealed and darted out from behind the counter. "I've been waiting forever to meet you!"

She got so close to Ronnie that I had to remind her of personal space. She mumbled something about big men and their women, but stepped back.

Ronnie, to her credit, just smiled at Jenny and said, "It's nice to meet you Jenny."

"You are so pretty, my God, Finn. I remember you telling me how pretty she was, but damn." Jenny threw a hand over her shoulder and waved at her father, who was barreling toward us.

"Jenny, personal space!" Kip said.

"Ugh!" Jenny threw her hands up, and Ronnie laughed. "Finn's already warned me, dad."

"We don't want to scare Finn's girl off the second she walks in the door, bug." He threw an arm over Jenny's shoulders and pulled her back a few steps.

"Ronnie, this is Kip. The owner, and my personal trainer, although he won't call himself that."

She took his hand and said, "Nice to meet you."

"Don't let us keep you, Cal is already in the back room messing with the stereo."

We said goodbye and promised Jenny we'd see her before we left for a shake. I took Ronnie's hand as we walked to where the classes took place. Kip had remodeled a few years ago to add more class rooms, and now the gym boasted four rooms each complete with walled mirrors, and hardwood floors.

Cal was setting out mats in near perfect rows, her long silver hair braided in a single rope down her back, flowing with her movements.

She looked up as she surveyed her work and smiled. "Finn! I didn't expect you today." She wrapped her arms around my waist and squeezed. When she pulled back she spotted Ronnie's hand in mine. "And you brought a partner!"

"I did, Cal, this is Ronnie. My..." I panicked for a moment, I didn't want to call her my baby mama, even though she was.

"I'm Ronnie, Finn's friend." She said, giving me a small smile.

"Well, I'm so happy to hear that, Kip and I are so happy for you two. We'll go easy today." She gave us a wink and shuffled us to put our shoes beside a mat.

We picked the last two mats closest to the opposite wall where the door sat. While we waited for the class to fill Ronnie fidgeted with her hair, pulling strands loose and twining them around her fingers.

Placing my hands on her shoulders I guided her to sit on the squishy mat. She let me rub her shoulders as the small class trickled in with other couples partnered up.

Cal called the class to their mats and we began with small smooth movements to open our bodies up. I watched Ronnie become more and more open to the stretches and felt a sense of pride swell.

Along with other, much more sensitive parts.

Ronnie's ass was up in the air, her shirt had slid up to her breasts and I felt the shift in my pants. Goddog. I shook my head and tried to avoid looking at the way her leggings fit her tightly across her ass.

Cal clapped her hands and instructed us to move our mats together. I had to readjust myself before we got into the moves that would bring our bodies closer together. I really didn't need Ronnie getting upset with me.

"Okay, our toppers, please lay back on the mat. Knees up, feet flat." I laid down, following Cal's instructions and waiting for the others to do the same. A few couples argued about who their top would or should be, and I caught Ronnie having to hide her smile.

I hit her ankle, and we shared a conspiratorial smile.

"Now, our bottom's. Please place one foot on either side of your partner's hips. Like this." Cal demonstrated with Kip below her, and Ronnie followed suit. I was confused about the sexual orientation of the session. But shrugged it off as Cal being intuitive to our other guests.

"Lower your body slowly to sit between your partner's legs, like a throne, if you will." Ronnie watched Cal move her body over Kip and situate herself on his crotch. "Once here, grip your palms on your partner's knees and rock your hips."

Ronnie's eyes flew to mine and I gulped. I obviously hadn't looked at the schedule close enough when I'd put our names down. I knew Cal and Kip offered Kama Sutra yoga for couples, but I didn't think to ask. Had I signed us up for sex yoga instead of prenatal yoga?

Fuck me, this was going to end poorly.

Ronnie

Twenty-Four

Kama Sutra yoga.

Just what I needed, horny, pregnant, with Finn looking hot as hell under me. I couldn't get my emotions to agree with me, I didn't know if I wanted to be mad, or uncomfortable. I just knew this was going to go either really well, or really, really bad.

I didn't sit slowly, instead I dropped like a sack of bricks on top of Finn. Instead of grinding on him like Cal instructed, I leaned down as much as my belly would allow and whispered, "You're so dead."

To his credit he looked ashamed, his cheeks were pink and I could tell he was trying hard not to look at me.

"I didn't know." He forced out as I sat up and joined the rest of the class as they moved. Cal was still instructing, telling us to move and find what works for us. How to utilize our partner's legs and torso.

I grinded on him, feeling him grow beneath me. I shot him a glare and he sent me a pleading look, mouthing, "I'm sorry."

We moved again, rolled is more appropriate. She instructed the 'toppers' to lift their shoulders and twist them and their partner's over so now I was flat on my back with my feet planted on the mat. Finn's knees were tucked under my ass, lifting it up so my hips were still aligned with his.

I hadn't been touched in months, and it stirred up the need I had, the hunger to be touched and lavished. To lose myself in orgasmic bliss with another person. An exchange of pleasure ripped from the bottom of your soul.

"Ronnie." Finn said my name sharply, and my eyes snapped open.

Oh God. No. I didn't.

Embarrassment flooded my system, my face was on fire, and Cal clapped. Fucking *clapped*. "If you're doing it right, that is exactly the response your body should have."

I closed my eyes and took a deep breath before looking up at Finn. He was no longer moving, instead he was staring down at me with questions I didn't have the capacity to answer.

"Are you okay?" Finn asked, gently untucking his knees from where my hips and ass rested.

I nodded, because of course I was okay. But my pride? That bitch flew out the window when I'd moaned in front of strangers.

Shame shouldn't take up space in my brain, I fucked Finn in a hall with no privacy for fucks sake. I should not be ashamed that I took pleasure from him. But in a room full of strangers...God I felt like a horny idiot.

We continued with the flow of class, barely touching each other, soft whispers of his skin on mine as he tried to give me space. When we had shifted into the cool down phase, Finn on his haunches and leg spread wide bracketing my body, I let him rub my shoulders.

He didn't speak as we finished and rolled our mats up to hand back over to Cal for cleaning. She beamed at us and commended us on a job well done. I tried not to cringe thinking about the job she was referring to.

Jenny met us at the shake bar back up near the front of the building. Her hair swayed as she bounced around behind the bar, filling blenders with customer orders.

"Hi, you two!" She yelled while starting three blenders in rapid succession.

We both gave her a murmured reply, something close to a hello. I climbed onto the bar stool and stared at the granite top.

"Rough yoga?" She laughed, and we both looked at each other.

"I'm really sorry." Finn whispered just loud enough that I could hear. "I should have looked at the schedule closer."

I laughed, because he *absolutely* should have. But also, I felt like this broke some of the tension riding between us. Finn joined me, and we laughed together. Jenny beamed at us, "Y'all are the most adorable couple."

"Oh we..." I started.

"Jenny..." Finn interrupted.

She lifted her arms in front of her, "Sorry, sorry. I know, it's complicated."

I raised my brows at him, how much of our lives did he share? It's like this place was his family. Like Billy's was mine.

I stared at him while he casually spoke to Jenny and Kip, who joined in on the ribbing. They conversed so easily, Finn's shoulders were relaxed, his smile easy and open. The burly man I met at Dusk 'Til Dawn, replaced by this carefree version.

"He's something, ain't he?" Jenny slid onto the stool beside mine with a pink shake, and slid it my way. "Strawberry, right?"

I nodded, and my brows kissed in the center as I stared at the shake. It didn't look the same as what Kip handed Finn. It looked colder somehow.

"Finn brought in strawberry ice cream the other day for you." She shrugged like it was a totally normal thing to request at a gym. "Said it was your favorite. And dad loves Finn, so ice cream stayed, even if you didn't come."

I couldn't bring the straw to my lips, my jaw hit the floor for a second. Who did that? Finn, that's who. He really was trying, in the ways he knew how. Like a milkshake instead of a protein shake that he knew I wouldn't drink.

"Thank you." I said to her, and she chatted away as I drank the shake. Either she was trying to distract me from my swirling thoughts, or she loved to talk. She told me all the dirt on the people who came through. Who to avoid, who to make friends with. As if she knew I was coming back.

Jenny stood to answer the phone at the check-in desk, Cal breezed through, swatting Jenny's bottom and telling her to get moving.

"What did you think of yoga this morning?" Cal asked as she got closer.

"It was something." I replied, "I didn't realize anywhere in town did Kama Sutra yoga."

She winked and said, "Oh, we do a lot of 'out of the normal' classes. You should come back for prancing with puppies!"

"What in the world is that?" I asked through giggles. It sounded absolutely ridiculous, and exactly like something I'd sign up for.

"It's less than Zumba, but enough to get your heart racin'. Plus we get with the local shelter and they bring in all the adoptable dogs to dance with us."

"You're kidding!" I said, forgetting all about my milkshake.

"It's a lot of fun, we have a pretty good turn out for it too." She grabbed her empty cup and tossed it in the trash. "Y'all should come."

When I turned, Finn was watching us with a big smile on his face. Which I returned, because I'd never felt this good at eight thirty in the morning. They were so welcoming and no one said a word about my many slip ups during yoga.

Pun intended.

"I should get you back." Finn declared. "Work stops for no one."

He helped me off the stool and after grabbing a few things we said goodbye to Jenny and Kip. They told me not to be a stranger, and that I could use Finn's membership anytime I wanted to visit. He feigned hurt, as if I would show up without him, and we headed out into the brisk morning air.

"You bought me ice cream, specifically for the gym." I sounded accusatory, but not unhappy. "You bought me gym ice cream!"

His smile was as radiant as I felt. We collapsed into our seats in the truck, laughing at the absurdity of our morning. He stopped laughing before I did and inhaled deeply before speaking, "I take it you like Wadey Weights?"

"I love it! Jenny is a ball of energy, and Cal and Kip seem like really good people."

He nodded, biting his lower lip. "I'm glad you came."

"I am too."

I surprised myself with the words, because I *did not* like to work out. But this morning wasn't half bad. I expected it to be worse, stuffy, formal, strict. Instead Cal and Kip made it fun and engaging.

Finn dropped me off at Fixin' To I Do with my bag of clothes for work tucked under my arm.

Before I closed the door I turned and found Finn's eyes on mine. "Thank you."

He smiled before he drove off, leaving me there with my thoughts churning.

Ronnie

Twenty-Five

Cravings for physical touch had always been my kryptonite. I knew this, and I understood it. I just didn't understand the constant need to get off recently. I wished I did, maybe my body would stop waging war with my brain over it.

This time the craving hit harder, and nothing I'd done was coming close to what my body was warring for. I'd tried the bathtub with the jets on and....nothing.

I had tried every trick I'd mastered while learning my body and nothing was coming close to the absolute *need* I had roaring through my body.

Feeling Finn grow beneath me yesterday had my already horny brain intensified to the point that I was about to come apart at the seams.

I debated calling the doctor, surely this wasn't normal for pregnant women to be this horny. However, I did not trust myself to keep cool, calm, and collected, and who wants their doctor to know that they're a fucking mess because they need to get laid?

My thoughts floated to the man who had starred in all of my fantasies since that dark hallway escapade. The way he took charge and whispered filthy words into my ear as he made my body sing with a fire I didn't know it could muster.

I knew I shouldn't, but the urge to call Finn was getting stronger. I knew that he thought I was with Eli, but I couldn't stop the hunger in my bones. With every passing second my body took over my common sense, and I found myself dialing the number I'd been loath to for weeks.

He answered on the first ring, as if he was staring at my contact too, just waiting for me to call. "Ronnie?" His gruff voice sent shivers over my body, nerves lighting up the fine hairs everywhere on my body.

"Can you come over?" I blurted, trying to hold in the pants of need in my chest. "Please, I-I need your help."

When he didn't answer my hopes sank and my libido revved up even more than I thought possible. I felt like I was going to come out of my skin with the need to orgasm.

Pregnancy hormones are no joke.

"I'll get back to you." He said, his voice sounded far away, as if he covered the speaker with a hand. Then the tale tale 'click' sounded in my ear as the phone call disconnected.

"Ughhh." I stomp my feet all the way to the couch. Exasperated and ready to combust. I couldn't even think about solo play anymore, it just wasn't enough and ended up frustrating me even more. I should have known he'd blow me off, just like he did before.

A knock on my door not long after I'd tossed my phone on the couch startled me and my robe fell open.

"Ronnie?" Finn's voice came through the thin door and I bolted up from where I'd collapsed rather dramatically. The floors suddenly felt too cold on my bare feet, when I made my way to the door.

Unlocking the door I pulled it wide open, forgetting my robe was open and exposing my very naked body to anyone in the hallway. Thank goodness Finn was a big ass man, because no one would be able to see around him anyway.

"Ronnie." He growled, as his eyes roamed my bump, the swells of my breasts.

"I need you." I whimpered, too keyed up to really care that I sounded like an absolute feral cat in heat.

I didn't care that he got here in a suspiciously quick time. Not when he groaned and pushed me back inside. Kicking the door shut with his boot he pulled my robe closed, securing the ties loosely and my pride took the kick straight to the heart. I knew he could see the way I needed this in the way my face fell and tears began to gather in my eyes. Frustration and regret were already taking up root in my soul.

"I know it's not fair for me to ask, but I really need this Finn." I couldn't stand this itching need burning inside me anymore. "Please, I nee--"

Finn gripped my hips and pulled my body into his, sealing his mouth over mine. I was shocked he'd given in so quickly, but I didn't fight it, because the way his lips felt moving against mine sparked tenfold.

My heart was beating at a furious pace and my throat worked double time making sounds of pleasure while my tongue tangled with Finn's.

He growled and flexed his fingers, delicious pressure burning through the fabric of my robe. I was soaked, practically a river of longing for him. I pushed my hands through his hair, tangling the waves between my fingers as he pulled me into his big, tattooed arms.

Walking us to my bed he didn't break the kiss as he maneuvered us gently down, his hands roamed over the cloth separating us, the heat of his palms felt like they burned straight through to my skin and I moaned into his mouth.

He pulled back, searching my face for any sign of refusal but he wouldn't find any. I needed this more than air, so I gave him a slight nod and a smirk to show him I was *so* okay with this.

He pulled gently on the ties of my robe that he'd just tied moments ago. Brushing the fabric from my shoulders he placed kisses there, trailing them down between my peaked breasts. He slowly moved down over the swell of my stomach, and whispered his lips over my hips. First the right, then the left, settling himself between my parted thighs with his gorgeous face hovering right above my pussy.

"Tell me what you need, Firecracker." His voice rumbled against my sensitive flesh at the apex of my thighs, right where I wanted him, and I mewled and squirmed, willing him to just *do* something.

"You, I need you to make me feel good." I whispered. His eyes flicked up to mine, and something passed between us, a truce...of sorts.

I caught the way one side of his lips tipped up before he was right on the target. He lightly licked my clit, teasing the sensitive bundle before sliding one of his thick fingers into my aching core.

"Goddamn." He practically moaned as he found me soaked and pliable.

He slipped another finger in as he sucked on my clit. My back arched off the bed with the utter bliss that was consuming my body. Like a burning star ready to flash and burn out.

"Yes!" I shouted as he continued to lap at my pussy, pushing the coil tighter and tighter through my muscles. It didn't take long for his expert fingers to curl and find the spot inside of my body that shut everything down and had me spiraling through an orgasm.

It felt white-hot and pulsing, my muscles contracted and tightened as release barreled through my whole being. My hands found their way back into Finn's hair as I kept him pinned there, and he murmured his approval by doubling down on his efforts, pushing me even higher than I'd ever been.

"Fuck me." I begged. If he didn't get into motion I was going to come again, and I'd had multiple orgasms enough times to know that the next one would be....messy. In the most luscious way.

He wasted no time shedding his clothes, pulling his belt out with one hand, at the same time he discarded his shirt with the other. Now gloriously naked he slid inside me, holding himself over my body. His tattoos rippled and moved as he thrust in and out slowly, building that mouthwatering friction again.

"Scream for me, Firecracker." He said as he moved faster, plunging deeper, fucking me harder. "Show me how much you need this."

His words brought a whole new wave of want through my bones. I was a sucker for his voice, and the way he played my body. The sounds he made as he pushed my body toward another mind shattering orgasm were nearly enough to send me over the edge.

"Finn." I growled as he slowed his pace again. Pulling out nearly to the tip before slowly, agonizingly slowly, pushing back in.

He leaned down, lips touching mine reverently, "That's not a scream, baby."

I writhed under him, trying and failing to meet his hips as he continued his shallow thrusts. He wouldn't give me any room to truly get the friction I sought.

"Damn it, Finn." I ground out.

His arms snaked behind my back, pulling me up, flipping our position. He settled on his back, against the pillows I'd propped on the wall as a makeshift headboard.

"Ride me, Firecracker." He said, lips turned up into a shit eating grin. "Take what you need."

I sank down on him, whimpering at being so full. The angle pushed him deeper, brushing the sensual spot inside of me that shot sparks to every nerve ending in my body.

"That's it, baby." He crooned, reaching up to cup my aching breasts. He rolled my peaked nipples between his fingers as I moved back and forth, rubbing my clit against his pelvis. My movements became frenzied as he brought his mouth to my nipple.

His tongue roamed over the delicate skin there, pulling and prodding my tight buds into his mouth, pushing me higher and higher into the ecstasy of passion.

"That's it, baby. Come all over my cock." He said as my muscles locked up and the peak of my climax tightened and released in a rush of fluid that coated his girth, just like he ordered. My legs were slick with my release, his hips shiny from my body's bliss.

Messy, just like I knew it would be, and oh so delicious.

He didn't allow me to stop moving, his arms wrapping around my body as he moved us both in sync with the waves of pleasure flowing from my body.

"Fuck yes." He said, burrowing into the space where my neck met my shoulder. He nipped the skin as I screamed out the last of my release and he finished deep inside of my body.

We rested there, completely spent, him going soft inside of my warmth. I let him hold me, because I'd missed this. The feeling of being loved, and *wanted*. He placed gentle kisses along my bare shoulder as I came down from the impeccable high.

My body was spent, my mind blissfully blank, and I felt like I could sleep for years.

Finn

Twenty-Six

Her body relaxed in slow, subtle movements.

I knew this wasn't what I wanted, no *needed* it to be, but I couldn't help the way it felt to be here with her. To share in the comfort of her space.

Her head fell onto my shoulder, mouth open and light puffs of breath stirred the hair that she turned loose in our frenzied kissing.

I didn't want to wake her, but I knew we both needed to get cleaned up, and I definitely needed to change her sheets. I whispered her name, gently shifting my body so I could look at her.

She murmured something and shifted in my arms, grinding back down on my already growing cock. Bad idea.

I slid to the edge of her bed, carrying her with me so I could slip out of her and move her to the couch.

"Stay." She muttered as I carried her to the couch. I didn't think she was aware enough to know what she was doing to me, but I didn't care at the moment.

"Shhh," I said, laying her out on the couch, "I'll be right back."

I stumbled around her apartment that couldn't be bigger than her office at Fixin' To I Do. As quietly as I could, I searched the bathroom cabinet for a spare set of sheets. When I didn't find any I searched all of the apartment, finding things I probably shouldn't be curious about, but definitely was.

Finally I found some sheets under the counter in her kitchen. She really needed to consider something bigger. Like the house I bought. What was she going to do when our baby came? Where would all of their stuff go? Babies had a lot of shit for such little humans.

As quickly as I could, I stripped the bed and remade it with the fresh sheets. Then I relieved myself in her bathroom and went in search of my underwear, figuring she wouldn't be too pleased to have me running around her apartment naked.

She was snoring softly on the couch when I pulled her into my arms and walked her to the bed. She didn't make a sound as I laid her down. Her thighs were shiny with her orgasm and mine, and as much as I fucking loved the sight,

I knew she would want to get as clean as she could before getting into the fresh sheets.

I headed back to the bathroom and ran a rag under the faucet, the water didn't get very warm and I wondered if her shower was the same way. This apartment sucked, and I started conjuring ideas on how to get her to move in with me.

Once I got the washcloth as warm as it would get, I lightly pushed her thighs apart and ran the cloth over her thighs and legs first, so I didn't scare her. She mumbled, but didn't squirm so I flipped the cloth over and ran it over the flesh of her pussy.

It was still dripping, so I decided to rinse the cloth and go over her once more. I didn't want her to get an infection or anything, I didn't understand the mechanics of it really, but I knew she should be somewhat clean after sex.

When I was satisfied with my work I placed the cloth on her tub to dry and slipped under the covers with her. If this was the only time I would get to cuddle Ronnie I'd selfishly take it.

I woke to the smell of chocolate and cinnamon. It was pleasant and at first it took me a minute to recognize where I was.

When my eyes landed on Ronnie, unfortunately fully clothed, she was watching me, sipping out of a mug of what I hoped was coffee, but knowing her was most likely hot chocolate.

"You stayed." She said, holding her mug against her chest like protection.

I nodded, because I told her I would. Because I wanted to prove to her that I wasn't going anywhere. I wasn't running, and if she'd let me explain, maybe she would understand.

Her lips twisted and she bit the inside of her cheek. I could tell from the way she sucked in the skin. "Why?"

"You asked me to." I answered, pulling myself out of her warm bed and slowly walking toward her. She halted my progression with a hand, and my heart sank a little.

"This can't happen again." She said, as if I should have known it. As if it was a given.

"Because you're afraid?" I asked, slapping myself internally for the way it came out. I'd meant to tease, but it came out more honest than I intended.

Her face scrunched, "And that right there, is why."

"Ronnie," I sighed, "I didn't mean it the way it came out."

"You did, and it's okay."

I shook my head, willing my thoughts to rearrange so I could salvage this. This fragile bond we had.

"Can we at least talk about it?" I asked, hoping that she would hear me out.

She shook her head and her old oven beeped obnoxiously. She placed her mug on the chipped counter and grabbed an oven mit. Pulling what smelled like spectacular cinnamon rolls out of the oven.

My mouth watered at the sight, but I couldn't eat one. The carbs alone would skyrocket me out of my daily macro limits and I'd have to hit the gym twice as hard.

Her shoulders were tight as she braced her arms on the counter after taking the hot buns out of the oven.

"We can't do that again." She repeated, back still turned to me.

"Why not?" I asked, because I knew she'd enjoyed herself. It was evident in the way she glowed even though she desperately wanted to deny it. The way she'd screamed my name as she came, the way she'd asked me to stay.

"Because, Finn." She turned and leaned against the counter, facing me. "We're having a baby, and I may trust you with my body, but I don't trust you with anything else."

Ouch.

"I can explain, if you'll let me." I said, completely at a loss, because she didn't know me, not like I wanted her to. "I promise if you give me the chance it will all make sense. Plus you're right, we are having a baby, don't you think we should at least try to be partners?"

"Partners?" Her face pulled into a saccharine smile. "You think we can be partners?"

"Why can't we?" I asked, genuinely puzzled. We could be great parents, we could be even better as *married* parents, but I didn't voice that.

"Because of what we just did." She hollered, throwing her hands up. "Because apparently pregnancy hormones make me horny as hell and my fingers and toys just don't work like your body does, and I can't get attached to you."

Her eyes hit the floor, and I couldn't help but wonder what she meant when she said she *can't* get attached to me. Then it hit me. She was sticking to her charade of a romance with 'surfer guy', even when I knew damn well she had no feelings for him.

She had to know that I could see right through her plan with, whats-his-name. That it wasn't real. But instead of coming clean, even though the fucking opportunity couldn't have been better, she was still trying to lie to me.

Herself too, if she wouldn't stop fighting *this*.

Us.

"Wow." I said, piecing it all together and feeling like the biggest fucking idiot on the planet. "Of course you can't, even though *you* called *me*."

Her eyes snapped up to mine and I saw it, the fear in her eyes. The unshed tears lining her lower lashes. The guilt.

"Don't worry, Firecracker." I spat, turning around to find my clothes, I couldn't even look at her as I got dressed and headed for the door. "I'll be your friend, but fuck how I feel right? Because I'm just the asshole that got you pregnant and ran."

Her lips pop open and her cheeks turn bright pink, but I didn't stick around to hear what she had to say. My feelings were hurt, and the only way I knew how to squelch them was a good workout.

I slammed the door on my way out, the whole building feeling like it vibrated with the force of my pain, and I almost winced.

Almost.

Ronnie

Twenty-Seven

I didn't have time to sit around and stew on Finn's words, as much as they haunted me. Even if I told him the truth about Eli, he wouldn't believe it. Did I need to tell Eli about what happened? We weren't a real couple so why the hell did I feel so sick to my stomach? I never wanted to be that girl, the one who lied to the people I cared about.

And I did, I fucking cared for Finn. It was terrifying, and electrifying all at once. I wanted everything with him, but I didn't want them for a fleeting moment. I wanted all of him, forever, and I had no idea if he was as invested as I was, I wouldn't survive it if he left again, my heart would shrivel up and I would no longer *live*.

I'd simply *exist*.

I couldn't give him that power over me. So whatever he thought when he left last night, while I knew it couldn't come close to my actual reality, maybe it was better if we stayed this way.

Bellamy called and woke me from the warmest rest I'd ever had. Which was why I decided to bake cinnamon rolls. Knowing he would not approve. With the "clean eating" thing he seemed to have going on.

Not that I was complaining about the way he looked, it got me hot just thinking about all the muscles packed onto that man. The way his stomach rippled and contracted while he moved above me. How I wanted to lick the veins that ran up his arms.

NO.

I couldn't go down that road, not only because I had a meeting with our current bride, but because Bellamy could read me like the back of her hand, and if I wasn't as picture perfect as I normally was, she'd know I did something I wasn't supposed to.

After scarfing down two cinnamon rolls—don't judge, I was eating for two—I raided my closet for something to wear. I really needed to go shopping for maternity clothes, I'd made it down to the wire now and really didn't have a choice.

My faithful leggings were uncomfortably tight, and I might have ripped a hole in them this morning when I couldn't get them over my swollen stomach.

That left me with the maternity dress Xavier picked up for me last week. He surprised me with it at our last game night, stating it was too perfect to pass up.

It was a simple dress, fabric loose and flowy. Covered in wildflowers and ruffled at the bottom. Standing in front of the mirror with my blond hair still curled from last night I felt almost alluring. Like the pregnancy glow had finally kicked in.

I paired the dress with a simple pair of brown flats that had the best cushion a girl could buy, and gold earrings to match my gold pendant of Athena that I never took off.

Grabbing my bag I shuffled the contents around for my keys, pulling them out and checking one last time that I had everything I needed before locking the door and heading for our shop. During our phone call she instructed me to go in through the back door.

We had to finalize some options for Stacey's bridal portraits coming up this weekend, and I really needed to answer emails I'd been putting off. I didn't like to hurt feelings, but in business we had to go with what we thought was best, and the current caterer just hadn't been doing so well the past two events we'd held.

Bellamy and I somehow swindled Billy into agreeing to cater Stacey and Garrett's wedding. We both knew he'd be great, and we were moderately sure that he would love it.

Finn's truck was in the parking lot, which wasn't completely out of the normal. But it did give me pause. He was undoubtedly still upset with me. I needed to tell him and Eli that things couldn't continue.

Bellamy was already in her office, I could hear her on the phone with one of our vendors for the upcoming wedding.

Making my way across the hall into her office, I took a seat and waited for her to finish. She hung up and went about her tasks for the day. I knew she was waiting me out, to see how long I'd wait before caving.

"I'm sorry." I said, feeling like a total jerk. "I didn't mean it."

She looked up from her computer and gave me a small smile. "I'm still your best friend, Ronnie."

"I know, and I shouldn't have gotten so upset. I told Finn I want to see the house. I'll even go today after our meeting with Stacey."

Shaking her head she said, "Did you at least hear what Finn had to say about the house?"

I don't think we actually talked about it now that she brought it up. "He had a plan?"

"Ronnie!" She chastised. "Y'all didn't even talk about it? Did you?"

I had the decency to look away, because we hadn't. I made a mental note to ask the first chance I got.

She gave me a cheeky look but didn't press further as she closed her laptop. "Stacey will be here in a few minutes. It's her last dress fitting before her portraits with Xavier."

"Speaking of, where is Xav?" I asked.

She waved her hand. "Flitting about, said he'd meet us at the shop."

I shrugged, that sounded like him. He was always busy, running around, working all hours of the day. I'd have to remind him it was my turn to host family game night, and that attendance was mandatory.

Tidying up the shop before Stacey arrived, I moved magazines and dusted the shelves. I was so lost moving around the space, and lost in my own thoughts that I didn't hear the doorbell. Stacey giggled and I immediately turned around and nearly shrieked.

"Sorry! I didn't mean to scare you."

I waved my hand back and forth as I caught my breath. "No problem." I squeezed out through pants.

Bellamy walked into the room, eyeing us suspiciously. "You okay?"

"I scared her," Stacey said.

She rolled her eyes and motioned us toward the door, where a sleek town car was pulled up. Bellamy and I both didn't like to drive, which was another concern for the house situation, but I'd save it for later Ronnie's problem.

We sat in the car, me in the front, Bell and Stacey in the back. The driver pulled away from the curb and headed to the same dress shop where we had taken Haven to get her dress. It was easily one of the most expensive items on Stacey's wishlist, but what our brides wanted, they got. Within reason.

She picked a simple gown that covered her from shoulder to wrist in ivory silk. The bust was a sweetheart neckline that complimented her long neck. It was a stunning dress with appliques that bordered the train.

"It fits like a glove!" Stacey crooned and I teared up.

She would be a stunning bride, which meant Eli would be leaving in two weeks. I needed to let him go, and focus my efforts on Finn. We were going to have a baby, sooner rather than later. It was high time I got my shit together and focused on the future of my child.

When we got back from the dress shop Xavier was waiting, sprawled out on our couches like he owned the damn place.

"Where have you been?" Bellamy started.

"Chill Bells, I had a lot of errands to run." Xavier said lazily. Recently he was either irritable or extremely happy. Looks like we got happy Xavier today.

"Our bride was expecting to meet you today." Bellamy almost growled, and I knew she was about to blow if I didn't intervene.

"I'm sure he has a valid reason for missing us today," I said, moving between the two. Xavier was glaring at Bell and she was lasering him with her eyes.

"I told you already, I had a lot of errands to run." He waved his hand in front of his chest as if shooing a fly.

"When we tell a client that you're going to show up, You. Show. Up." Bell stepped forward. "Or do we need to find another photographer that wants our business?"

"Okay, Bell." I said, pushing her toward her office.

"I can't believe you!" Xavier exclaimed, standing from the couch.

Her face flushed red, and I knew we were about to get very angry, Bell. "You can't believe me?" She huffed and got all up in his face. "You're the flake here. It's our first client on our own, and *now* you want to start not showing up?"

Xavier had the decency to look ashamed, like he didn't think of it that way. Once Bell put it into perspective like that, I could rationalize her anger. Xavier sat down with a sigh and said, "I'm sorry. I didn't mean to flake on y'all."

"Xavier, what's been going on with you recently?" I asked, making my voice soft. "You've been... distant."

He shuffled his feet on the carpet, but didn't say anything. Bellamy sat down on his other side and I followed suit, squishing him between us.

"I went to see a therapist." He squeaked out.

"That's great news!" I told him. Therapy had saved my tail a time or two. Bellamy didn't speak, instead she let Xavier have his space to feel whatever he was feeling.

"Since Landon came back it's been bringing up a lot of memories." His eyes watered but he didn't cry. "The session went over, it won't happen again."

"Well, my thoughts still stand, but now I feel slightly like a dick." Bell huffed.

"You are a dick." Xavier quipped back.

We all laughed because she may be an ass sometimes, but she was the fiercest friend.

"Don't shut us out. You need us, just as much as we need you." I said, because even though we were all laughing now, he needed to know how serious I was.

He nodded, dabbing a tissue under his eyes and nose to clear up anything that had dripped. We chatted for a few more minutes and just enjoyed the company. Bellamy and I had a few things to catch up on so we headed to our offices and bid Xavier goodnight.

Bellamy locked the door behind him and we silently made our way to our offices. I turned my lights off because it was easier with just the table lamp light this late. I tried stifling a yawn, and failed miserably when I heard Bellamy across the hall saying, "None of that!"

I answered a few emails and approved a new mock-up for our redesigned logo. It was perfect, a blend of Bell and I. Our tastes may not be the same, but we meshed seamlessly.

I caught myself drifting, eyes heavy as the words on paper blurred. I'd just rest my head on the table for a second, then I could get back to work.

Finn

Twenty-Eight

My phone rang as I was climbing out of the shower. I was going to miss the upgrades my penthouse in the city had. The house didn't have the sleek lines and marble my apartment did, but it also didn't have the cold and detached feel.

Bellamy's face was lit up on my screen but went black once the ringing stopped. Alarm thrummed through my system. Bellamy never called me, Aaron did. Dripping wet I unlocked my phone and immediately dialed back.

"What's happened? Is Ronnie okay?" I blurted the moment she answered, not even giving her any time to say 'hello'.

"Easy, big guy. Everything is fine." Bellamy said by way of greeting. "Wouldn't want you to break a nail, punching numbers so fast."

Sometimes it was easy to see why Ronnie loved her, this was not one of those times.

"What's wrong?"

"Nothing is wrong, I just said that."

"Then why are you calling me?"

I could hear Aaron telling Bellamy to give him the phone, and her grumbling something about a big overprotective teddy bear.

"Hey man, Ronnie fell asleep at her desk." My best friend's voice filled my speaker. "I would normally take care of it. But Bell and I have that *thing* we have to do."

Right. That thing, for the baby shower Ronnie doesn't know anything about. "I'm on my way."

Drying off as fast as I could, I dressed and grabbed the essentials. Rationally I knew they wouldn't leave her alone, mainly because I didn't have a key, but also because she was pregnant, and that was just a common courtesy thing.

The drive wasn't terrible this time of evening, everyone was settling down ready for bed. I should chap her hide for working this late, especially with only fifteen weeks left of her pregnancy.

I made it in time to see Aaron and Bellamy making out against the side of the brick building they leased.

"Get a room." I hollered, cupping my hands around my mouth.

Aaron laughed and clapped me on the back when I approached. Bellamy however opened her mouth to reply when Aaron wrapped his hand around her mouth and snuffed whatever the snarky comment would have been.

Her eyes went to slits and it was my turn to laugh.

"I'll get her home safe." I vowed. "Y'all go do that thing you have to do."

The back door was propped open, letting in the cool spring air. I knew where Ronnie's office was, but I was not prepared for the sight of her asleep on her desk.

Her head was on a pile of paperwork, the slope of her back led to her ass sitting on a rolling chair that looked like she was currently about to fall out of.

The room was small, so maneuvering her without waking her up was going to be impossible. She mumbled a little as I gently shook her shoulder, but didn't even crack an eye.

"Ronnie..." I said, rocking her a little harder. "Firecracker. Wake up."

She cursed and turned her head. Gentle snoring filled the room as I looked for another way to get her out. I could lift her, but I didn't know if I could get around the desk with us both.

I was out of options, and decided to go for it.

Rounding her desk I made a mental note to talk to her about late nights. She couldn't keep this up, not only for our baby, but also for her health.

She thought I didn't notice the extra effort it took for her to stand for longer periods of time, shifting her weight from foot to foot.

Looping my arm under her legs I flipped her legs up, and caught her back with my other arm. She was a featherweight in my arms, snuggling deep into my shoulder. Hell, I could get used to this.

She kept mumbling things as I adjusted her perfectly in my arms. When I had her settled, I maneuvered my way around her desk, being sure to avoid hitting her head against the wall. After I made it out of her office, I walked her straight to my truck and tucked her into the backseat where she could lay down.

Quick as I could, I locked the place up with her set of keys I'd picked out of her purse, remembering to grab the rest of her things. The drive wasn't long, and the doorman let us in since I couldn't find her key to get into the actual building.

I held her as I waited for the elevator to open, and all the way up into her apartment. I tried a few different keys, why did she have so many fucking keys? I shifted her so I could unlock the door once I found the right one.

She stirred and mumbled something, eyes blinking open and shut.

"Shh." I said, gently sitting her on her feet so I could get the damn key in the lock. "I've got you."

When I had the door unlocked and could gently kick it open I gathered her back into my arms, and carried her in.

It smelled like the first surf on the beach, like sunlight over salty water. Settling her onto the mattress I found her blankets and covered her up, taking a moment to just look at how beautiful she was. She had this glow about her that I wanted to bottle.

I didn't want to leave. The couch wasn't my ideal accommodations, but I'd make due. I had let my temper get the better of me the last time I was here, and I knew that wouldn't earn me any brownie points.

I needed Ronnie on board for the house. She deserved it, so I committed to finally convincing her to move into the new house.

I must have passed out at some point because her coffee machine was brewing and the sun was streaming in through her windows.

"Good morning, pretty boy," Ronnie said walking from the bathroom in only a towel.

I had to rearrange myself before getting up.

"Good morning." I had to clear my throat a few times, morning thickness made me grumble. "Sorry, I didn't mean to stay the whole night, but I didn't want to leave after carrying you to bed."

Her slight shoulder hunch had me tripping over my next words. "No...what I meant,"

I sighed. "I meant, you fell asleep at the office, and I didn't want to take a chance on anything happening if I left you alone."

Her shoulders loosened, and I felt a sense of relief watching it happen. I was trying to learn the best way to speak to her. My parents had been helping. With all their therapy talk, sometimes I thought they were psychoanalyzing me.

Ronnie had left her hair down, the blonde waves shifted across her back as she moved. I sat back down, watching her gathering bits and pieces of clothing she deemed good enough to wear.

"Thank you."

It was said so softly, almost like a whisper she didn't want me to hear.

I nodded, but didn't trust my words not to fuck up this fragile moment, so I got up and used the bathroom, making sure to take long enough so she could change.

Ronnie

Twenty-Nine

"We need to talk about the house." Finn said as he emerged from the bathroom.

I was glad he gave me time to sort through all of the emotions I had going through my head.

"The house you've already bought?" I snarked.

"I should have talked to you first," he said, hands out beside his head, fingers splayed wide like a criminal caught in the spotlight. "But, I also wanted it to be a surprise."

"Surprise!" I replied, waving my hands. "I bought a house for all of us to live in, but it's okay because your best friend lives next door!"

He had the decency to recoil. "I admit, I didn't think it through."

I huffed and threw my hair over my shoulder before grabbing a mug and filling it with coffee.

"You can move into the house, and I can stay in the city. Or I can move in here, and we can take it slow."

"You're assuming there is a chance for a "we" at all." I hated being so hot and cold with him. But I couldn't bring myself to finally give into the feelings I had for Finn. Especially since he didn't even know the deepest darkest parts of my soul.

His face crumpled, but he recovered quickly. He crossed the room in two powerful strides, his impressive form moved like liquid.

"I can wait, take all the time you need, Firecracker."

His hands brushed my face, thumbs moving over my cheekbones before pulling away and heading toward the door.

"I'll have the movers here to pack up your stuff today."

I couldn't process his words. Like his touch short circuited my brain.

As promised, movers knocked on my door around lunch, just as I was heading out to run some errands with Bell for the shop. They handed me a form with my name on it, and the new house address.

I hadn't even seen the house yet!

"Hold on." I said, stopping the guy in front before he could barrel though my door. "I need to make a call."

"Okay, Miss Gibson."

I dialed Finn's number, his laugh came through my speaker first before he said, "I told you I'd have them there later."

"I don't even know where they're taking my stuff!"

"Put some shoes on, Firecracker, and come outside."

He hung up on me. Bastard.

I ran to my window, thankful for the first time ever that it faced the street. There he was, leaned back against his truck, arms tucked over the other, his legs crossed. He looked delicious as sin. My personal sin, covered in ink and muscles.

Congratulations

Your baby is the
size of an eggplant.

Finn

Thirty

I was so fucking excited to show her the house. I knew we still had some things to talk about, Eli being one of them, and our relationship being the next, but that could wait.

Seeing the surprise and utter joy on her face as we made our way to our new home was indescribable. It was nestled in a cul-de-sac, next door to Aaron and Bellamy, who just so happened to be moving in today as well.

Ronnie squeaked when she spoke. "Bell!"

She ripped out of the car faster than I had ever seen her move, especially being pregnant. Her belly was getting rounder, and I had read that babies could be felt by others at this stage. I wanted to hold her while our baby moved inside of her.

She glowed as her hair bounced around on top of her head. Overalls the color of denim covered her from shoulder to ankle. But the legs were tiers of ruffles. Ronnie never ceased to dress in odd clothes.

I walked over to Aaron while Bellamy showed Ronnie their place. Content to wait with my best friend and breathe for a moment before showing Ronnie the many reasons I bought this house.

"We should be able to open up in the next few weeks." Aaron said when I clapped his shoulder. He'd been working hard on his newest endeavor, and he deserved all the success he was going to have.

"That's great, man."

"We're never gonna hear the end of being neighbors," Aaron said as the girls chattered on somewhere inside the house.

"Yeah." I agreed. Secretly I loved it though. Aaron found these two properties before they were done, and when we saw them, we knew. This would be it for our girls. It wasn't far from their office, and it was even closer to the big city.

It was the perfect in-between.

The girls came spilling out through the garage that would only house Aaron's truck for now. Ronnie swayed over to me, resting her hand on my elbow.

"Can I see it now?" Her face turned up toward mine, blue eyes shining so bright in the afternoon sun.

I nodded and we strolled to the newly laid sidewalk that connected the whole little neighborhood. The walk up to the house was laid with tulips that would bud soon. The house was a modest two story white vinyl home.

With a double wood door stained a walnut brown, the windows gave the interior the best lighting, and columns that closed in the porch finished off the curb appeal.

Her eyes bounced around and she stopped, trying to take in everything, all the details so she could burn into her mind. I watched her step up onto the porch and take a deep breath before twisting the handle.

She stepped inside, slipping off her faithful flip flops she'd grown accustomed to. Leaving them on the concrete by the door as she padded around. Her feet ghosting over the carpet in the living room.

Tracing her finger over the fireplace mantel, she kept her back to me, and I let her have her space to just take everything in. She walked past the shelves that lined the wall beside the fireplace into the dining room.

The walls had all been painted a light gray, the trim a bright white. I didn't have them furnish the space, I figured she would want to do that.

She floated through the dining room into the back entryway that led to a big backyard that eventually would have a pool. Under the stair storage was across from the back door and then the kitchen took up the bottom half of the house.

It was open to the living room, separated just a bit by the stairs that led to the bedrooms. Everything was stainless steel, and bright white cabinets. Black and white marble topped every surface, and I knew that she would want to paint the cabinets.

Her face was splotchy, pink dotted her cheeks and her eyes were glassy.

I didn't speak as I made my way over and wrapped her in my arms. She cried, shoulders shaking and breaths choppy.

"Firecracker?"

She just shook her head against my chest and cried. We stood there long enough for the sun to start to turn the sky bright orange, and the crickets to chirp.

"I can't." She hiccuped and tore out of my arms, pivoting and heading for the front door. In two strides I caught her arm, gently wrapping my fingers around her bicep. I turned her around, tears continued to pour from her eyes as she sobbed.

"Tell me what's going on." I pleaded, "I want to be here, I think I've made that very clear."

She nodded, but didn't move to speak.

"Please, Firecracker."

I'd get down on my knees if I thought it would help. But I needed her to want to tell me whatever it was that was keeping her from finally giving us a chance.

"I'm the reason I have no family." Her voice broke on the last few words.

"I don't understand."

"I killed my family, Finn!" She screamed and fell to the floor.

Ronnie

Thirty-One

There it was, my ugly truth.

Laid out at his feet. He knelt down in front of me and lifted my body from the floor. He cradled me in his arms as he got situated on the floor. His back against the wall, me in his lap, tears and snot leaking from my face onto his shirt.

"Firecracker, look at me."

Guilty and full of sorrow, it was overwhelming, and I knew if I looked at him he would be waiting for more. For me to bare my soul to him now that I'd given him the biggest piece of my past.

"It's a long story." I sobbed.

"I've got nothing but time, baby." He said, stroking my cheek with his thumb.

I bit the inside of my cheek and took a deep breath. If I was going to do this I had to look at him. When I looked up, his eyes were open and waiting. Patient and unmoving like a lighthouse searching for its lost love.

"I have a lot to tell you, it's not pretty, and I wouldn't blame you if you didn't want to stick around after I tell you everything."

His eyes never left mine, as if he was hanging on every word I had to say.

"I'll respect your decision no matter what. I swear." He nodded, giving me the go ahead. "My mother and brother, Lucas, died in a car accident when I was sixteen."

My voice cracked as I continued telling the only other person on the planet I trusted about my darkest moments. "I was driving, I had just gotten my license and begged to drive us to meet dad in the city for a celebratory dinner. Mom relented, even though Lucas normally drove everywhere. He was so proud of me, he handed me the keys and we took off. I was so happy, singing along to the radio with my brother. I didn't see the truck merge lanes on the highway, they clipped the front bumper of our car, and we flipped. I don't know how I survived, all I remember is waking up in the hospital with my dad hovering over me, eyes swollen and void of emotion."

"Baby," Finn started, leaning toward me. But I had to keep going, I couldn't stop, he had to know everything.

"He took me home a few weeks after that, the hospital wouldn't release me due to my injuries and the way I handled my dad telling me my mother and brother died in the accident. He was never the same, the house was a mess,

I remember cleaning up as much as I could before heading to bed. Lucas's room was still the way it was when we left for dinner. Like a shrine just for him. I fell asleep crying in his bed. Dad got worse, he fell into depression, explosive episodes of grief. And it was my fault, I killed my family."

Finn gripped my hand with his free one, squeezing. Then he moved back, palm circling over my–*our*–baby. My breath caught, it was the most comforting gesture that tears flowed again. I didn't deserve the comfort, the warmth of his strong arms around me.

"I might as well have killed him too. He would get so angry, the night he hit me was the worst, and the last night I saw him alive. He knocked me into the floor and I hit my head on our fireplace. When I woke up the house was on fire and he was just sitting in his recliner, staring at a picture of all of us together. I begged him to get up, to leave with me. But it was like he couldn't hear me. Like he didn't *want* to hear me. A firefighter pulled me away from him and out into the fresh air. I didn't realize the smoke I had inhaled until they put an oxygen mask over my face. They wouldn't let me back into the house. No matter how much I protested and fought. I watched my house burn down with my father in it. They couldn't go back in, they had tried but the fire was too bad."

I couldn't look at him anymore. Shame and regret built in my stomach and threatened to spill over. "I killed my family, Finn."

A tear hit our joined hands, my eyes whipped up to his face, he was crying. "God, Ronnie." He said, voice stuck on my name. "I can't imagine the pain you've been carrying."

He shifted me in his arms, and held me tighter as we cried together. He let me mourn the loss of my family at the front door of our new house.

"I'm not going anywhere, baby." He murmured while we wept.

The scariest thing was, I believed him.

Finn

Thirty-Two

I let her cry, let her get out all of the things she had been bottling up for so damn long. I didn't know how long we sat there. It was dark by the time she wiped her eyes and we journeyed upstairs.

She crashed on the floor as I made a phone call to the movers. Explaining that they could go ahead and bring in the essentials from her apartment, but to be as quiet as possible. It was late and I offered them double their regular rate to move the rest in tomorrow morning.

They arrived soon after I called, moving her bed up the stairs and into the guest room. I had bought a king size suit that was waiting in the garage.

The front man agreed to move it up the stairs with me so I could put Ronnie to bed instead of letting her sleep on the floor any longer than she had to.

We got everything ready within an hour so I could transition her. She moved very little as I picked her up and transferred her to the bed. I took the band out of her hair, letting her long strands fall in a halo around her.

I pulled the blankets up around her shoulders and took a moment to place my hand on the swell of her stomach, rubbing circles over our baby. Earlier, it hit me that I hadn't done it before, that it was truly the first time I'd felt the little one we made.

Aaron came over with Bellamy not long after I had put Ronnie to bed. We helped the movers get everything off the truck and into the house.

"She's upstairs, the last bedroom on the left." I told Bellamy.

She nodded and kissed Aaron before heading up and disappearing around the corner.

"That was fast." Aaron commented.

"Yeah." I said noncommittally. I honestly still didn't know if she wanted to move in by herself, or if she would allow me to move in with her. "Let's put this stuff in her room."

"You aren't planning on sharing the master?"

"I am if she'll let me. But that extra bedroom? I'm gonna make it her closet."

He nudged my shoulder, and smirked.

We got everything moved and somewhat placed in organized chaos. The house already felt like it was home, and we didn't even have all of it furnished. Aaron brought beer over from his house next door and we cracked them open on the front porch.

"So." Aaron started.

"I don't know." I answered. "I'm all in, man. I think I've been in love with her for a lot longer than I want to admit."

I thought I saw him smile, but it was hard to see considering the street lights weren't working yet on this new street, and it was well past ten o'clock.

"I knew it." He laughed, "I mean, anyone with eyes can see y'all need each other. Even if you weren't in the situation you are with the baby, you just...work."

"I'm still mad that she won't let me know if it's a boy or a girl."

He chuckles, "Get used to it, brother."

We sat there, sipping our beers and enjoying the balmy night air. Only a few more months until our baby arrived and I resolved myself to make Ronnie see what our future could be, despite her tragic past.

Ronnie

Thirty-Three

I woke up in a tangle of navy sheets and the overalls I'd worn yesterday. The room looked eerily like the master in the house Finn bought. As the sleep fog cleared away, and I shuffled to the attached ensuite to relieve my bladder, memories from last night began solidifying.

I'd told Finn. My deepest fear and darkest memories.

I'd told him everything.

One glance in the mirror as I washed my hands and all of those thoughts were confirmed. My blue eyes were rimmed in pink, and purple bags hung under my eyes.

"I am a mess." I told my reflection.

I heard a deep chuckle at the door and spun around. Finn had one shoulder leaned against the door frame, tattooed arms crossed over his chest. "You're beautiful."

I scoffed and rolled my eyes. He smiled even brighter and nodded toward the bed. I huffed, but complied. Hopping up onto the bed and sitting with my legs crossed under me. He sat with one leg propped on the corner, the other supporting his weight on the floor.

"The movers will be here in a few minutes," he started, "and I haven't moved any of my stuff in, but I'd like to fill the baby room with essentials together."

"Okay."

"And if you're okay with it, I'd like to move some of my stuff into the guest room." He said it with such hope in his eyes that I couldn't help but nod and bite my lower lip.

"How did you like the bed?" He switched topics. "Was it comfortable?"

I laid my hand over his. "Finn," I said, snaking my head to catch his eyes, "It was a perfectly acceptable bed. You don't have to keep buying me things."

"I just want to give you everything, Firecracker. You deserve the world"

I hid my face, because I had to tell him. If I was going to really embrace this, with him, he had to know. "It wasn't real."

"What?" His brows kissed, in a damn near perfect v.

"I was never with Eli." I admitted.

He laughed, throwing his head back and patting his chest. "You really know how to stop a man's heart, Ronnie."

"What's so funny?"

"I know. Well I didn't at first." Finn chuckled darkly, like he knew this news would shock me. "Eli felt bad for me after the run in at Billy's. Told me the whole story."

"That little snake!"

"What can I say, men stick together." He mocked.

I smacked his stomach and he gently brushed my bangs from my face, pausing before he asked, "Can I please kiss you now?"

At my timid nod he dipped his head and lightly brushed my lips with his.

The kiss wasn't heat filled passion. Instead it was a comfort.

A promise, and that was so much sweeter.

Ronnie

Thirty-Four

Fake breaking up with Eli was fun. He took me to play mini golf, which he absolutely killed. We laughed, he fed me snacks and we talked about the wedding.

He loved his brother so much it almost brought me to tears hearing him tell me stories about them as children. How they would fight over girls, when they cried over their mom passing. It felt like something I should have had with my brother.

In a way Eli helped me with more than just keeping Finn at a distance. Guarding my heart and head from the possibility of a broken home wasn't helping me, it was holding me back.

He helped me want to love again. Especially since Finn had listened to my past and hadn't taken off the other night.

I wanted a family full of laughter and love, a whole heart and home. Finn wanted to be a father, and I knew he wanted to be a family with me and our baby. I could admit that the platonic friendship wasn't working out, even before I'd called him in that vulnerable moment.

We had connected in that hallway with my skirt skimming my ass and his hands skewing my top to hold on to my breast. I'd buried my hands in his thick hair, and my lips had devoured his. We had claimed each other that night.

Denying it now seemed pointless.

Finn and I could never be just friends.

But we could be family. He and I could build again, slowly this time. As co-parents and, hopefully...more.

"I hope Finn makes you happy, Ronnie." Eli said as we handed in our putters and left the cute place.

I ducked my head and blushed, because I knew Eli was sincere. He had been since the first time I'd met him.

"I think he will," I replied. Because even though my head saw the changes in him, my heart wasn't ready to admit it. I was sad to see Eli go, but since his sister's wedding was officially over he had no reason to stay.

He dropped me off at my apartment, where I had not thought to tell Eli I didn't live anymore. Just as I was pulling out my phone to call Finn for a rescue I heard his voice call out across the street.

"Need a ride, Firecracker?" I turned, finding the man himself leaning out of his truck window. "I think standing outside of a building you don't live in is called loitering."

I laughed and ran across the street to jump into his truck.

As he drove I imagined painting the nursery, decorating and putting furniture together. Finn would most likely get mad and call Aaron to come help, while Bell and I sat and enjoyed watching them work.

The laughter that would fill a house with no ghosts to linger or bad memories to surface. I could finally have a home, a real home to make warm and loving.

We laughed together as he drove us home.

The next morning Xavier called.

"Hey baby mama!" He shouted through the small speaker of my phone. "What are you up to today?"

I looked at Finn across the living room, he looked scrumptious in the mornings. Sweatpants hung low over his narrow hips, abdominals on full display as he made himself a morning shake.

"Finn and I are going furniture shopping."

"Oooo!" He screeched. "I'll be there in...well, send me the address and I'll be there when I get there!"

I laughed when he hung up and informed Finn of the change in our plans, watching in glee as his face transformed into a scowl. He did not like this idea. I texted Xavier the address. While we waited, Finn drank his shake and I had my morning *decaf* coffee.

It was one of the things Finn insisted I try for two weeks. I'd agreed, stupidly.

I hated decaf.

He may have laughed at my grumbling, and I may have kicked him in the shin. He kissed the top of my head and downed the rest of his shake before taking the steps two at a time up to where he'd been crashing at night.

Pouring my half cup left into the sink I followed, though not as fast considering the belly. Baby was strong and kicking all the time now.

Finn feeling our little bean move inside of me was one of the most precious moments of my life. The way his eyes went round at the little elbow our baby threw at his hand. Watching his eyes glaze over with happy tears.

It was a memory I never wanted to forget.

I was at the shop with Bell, ready to eat and waiting for Finn and Aaron to show up. We'd decided to have lunch together because Bell and I hadn't had much time with each other since all the baby shenanigans had started. Then Aaron had called and Bell told him our plan, so naturally they decided to tag along.

"I'm going to die of hunger." I groaned from my lounged position on the waiting room couch, which had become one of my favorite rest spots.

Bell laughed, "Whatever will we do?"

"You aren't allowed to make fun of me." I whined. "This baby is moving so much today, I swear there isn't enough room for my little bean."

The bell above the door chimed, and in strutted the bro pair.

"About damn time!" I shouted, "I'm wasting away here."

They both laughed and I curled my hands into fists.

"Easy, Firecracker." Finn said, kneeling by my upper half. "Baby giving you hell?"

I nodded, while also pouting. He laid his large hand on the swell of my stomach and immediately, as if our baby knew who it was, kicked his hand, hard*. "Ouch." I grumbled. But the room was silent, everyone's eyes were on Finn as he teared up, running a hand over his eyes a few times to clear them.*

"I..." He began, clearing his throat to try again. "Can I?"

His eyes snapped down to where his hand hovered over my stomach and back to my face.

"Was that the first time you felt them move?" I asked, sure that it had happened before.

He nodded, and smiled when our baby elbowed his hand again, nudging the stretched skin across my abdomen.

"Hi, baby," his voice cracked, "I'm your daddy."

Ronnie

Thirty-Five

Xavier pulled his little red car right up in the driveway, threw open the door, and promptly hollered. "Ohhhhhh this is nice!"

I could hear him from inside the door. If we had neighbors other than Bellamy and Aaron they wouldn't need an alarm clock. I opened the front door, ready to scoot him inside.

He stood there, looking between our two houses and said something to himself. I couldn't quite hear it, but I watched his mouth move.

"You comin', or what?" I laughed.

He moved then, hips twisting and arms pumping. He wrapped his arms around my shoulders and crushed my body to his.

"Hey, baby." He said rubbing my stomach. We stood there for a moment, until Finn came out with my flip flops and asked if we were ready.

Once we were settled in the truck, me in front with Finn and Xavier in the back, Xavier started firing questions.

"What kind of look are we going for? Or is it more of a *vibe* you want?"

I looked at Finn, it was his house after all.

"What?"

"Are you going to answer?" I asked.

"I figured you would."

"It's your house." I whispered.

Finn pulled the truck into the closest parking lot and put it in park. When he turned to me I shrunk a little in my seat.

"Uh...Finn,"

"No." He put up a hand effectively silencing my words. "It's *our* house, Firecracker. And I do not want to hear you say otherwise again. Understood?"

My eyebrows must have kissed my hairline with how shocked I was. Finn always had a dominating presence, but hot fucking damn. That was...

"Fucking hot." Xavier blurted, as if he'd read my mind.

Finn turned in his seat giving him a glare, "And you,"

Oh no, I felt like I needed to say something, to save Xavier from whatever Finn was about to unleash, but he surprised me again by saying, "Whatever you do, don't let her hold back. I'm buying whatever she wants. No matter the cost."

If I could have seen Xavier I would bet money that he had his hand on his chest, like it was trying to pound out of it.

I had to admit, it was sexy as fuck seeing Finn attempt to get along with my friends, and get stern with me. A girl could get used to that.

The furniture store Finn drove us to was enormous. Bigger than some showrooms Bell and I had been to for bridal events. They had sections for all of the rooms of a house.

Even pool houses, guest houses, dog houses. Who the hell bought this stuff just for dogs?

Rich people.

There was no way I would pay for anything in this store on my own. There weren't even price tags on items! Just serial numbers and color coded stickers. That's when I knew shit would be pricey.

The showroom floors all boasted different styles. From modern to eclectic, farmhouse to industrial. There was so much to look at I didn't know where to start.

We stood there for a few minutes, Finn at my back, Xavier to my right.

"Holy furniture." Xavier mumbled.

Finn chuckled and grasped my hand. Threading our fingers together he led us toward the first display of bedroom suits.

"You didn't get to pick the furniture in your room. If you don't like it you can get a different set."

"Finn." I said, pushing Xavier away from us. "We need to talk about this."

Xavier picked up on my not so subtle hint and began searching the other bedroom options.

"Ronnie, I thought we went over this."

"No, no." I said, wiggling a finger back and forth between us. "I told you I wanted you in the master bedroom with me and *you* said I was being rash, who uses that word anymore? Then I threw a spoon at your head and went to bed." I sighed, "This conversation needs to happen Finn, and I need you to hear me."

He looked straight into my eyes searching for something. "You don't have to..."

"I'm not." I interrupted. "I want to try, with you. I want to try *us*."

It was his turn to be surprised. He raised his eyebrows and ran his other hand over his face. "I don't want to rush you."

"It's a little late for that, party boy." I laughed and squeezed his hand.

He dipped his head down and kissed my forehead, it was sweet, and I felt like a princess when he pulled back and looked at me like I was the moon in his sky.

Ronnie

Thirty-Six

Shopping wore me out, physically, emotionally, and mentally. Finn and I had made a pretty big leap. Sharing a room and sleeping together, without actually having sex felt more intimate than I'd ever been with anyone.

Ever.

Xavier skedaddled soon after we got back to the house. I was grateful considering I had fallen asleep on the way back, only to be woken up by Xavier declaring his departure.

Finn side eyed him with a death glare as I blinked my eyes open. He helped me out of the truck and didn't let go of my hand until he tucked me into the bed. The furniture we'd picked out wouldn't be delivered until later today, and I wanted to be awake for it.

Afternoon sun filtered in through our curtainless windows when I opened my eyes. I could hear the hum of a truck in the driveway and threw the covers off.

As fast as my pregnant ass could safely go, I flew down the stairs, watching the people unload all of our new furniture. It was surreal that this was my life.

That Finn was here, directing the movers where to go, grunting at them when they started in the wrong direction. Drills were fired up, their whir causing my eyes to shift. Curtains were being hung, a beautiful cream velvet that I found at a second hand store I begged Finn to take me into.

We found just enough panels to hang on the front windows downstairs. I was so excited I almost peed myself, or maybe that was the baby kicking again.

I squealed a little, drawing Finn's attention. His smile spread and I gave him a goofy one to match. Finn must have a direct number to Big-People-R-Us because the movers were huge. I couldn't help trying to watch all of them.

Finn's arms slid around my belly, lifting it slowly and giving my body a much needed break. I sighed as he held my baby belly and leaned his chin on the top of my head.

Two of the movers brought in the dining room table I'd chosen, a vintage wooden piece that had been refinished. The scrollwork on the legs is what sold me. Flowers that reminded me of Finn's tattoos were carved into the surface, vines trailed up the legs and gripped the top that was glossy and black.

My eyes trailed after another mover, this time a woman, who brought in the entertainment center in three pieces. Book shelves lined the upper half with room for the television in the center, and cabinets finished off the bottom. She drilled them all together and into the wall before turning and starting on another project.

"Is everything how you envisioned it would be?" Finn whispered in my ear.

I nodded, "Even better."

Once everything was in the house and the movers had all gone, we settled in the nursery, where I sat in the new rocking chair Finn insisted we buy. He leaned against the door frame, watching me as I ran a hand absentmindedly over my bump.

"Penny for your thoughts?"

"We're doing this." I stated. "We're really giving this a try."

He nodded, and his eyes crinkled in the corners. "We really are."

"Xavier wants to do maternity pictures with us."

"Okay," he said, stepping into the room. "Is that what you want?"

"I want a lot of things."

He offered me his hand and I took it. Helping me up from the cloud-like chair he held me there resting his hand on the top of my belly. Just two parents, looking into each other's eyes.

"Are you ready for bed?" Finn rumbled.

I nodded and trailed after him, hand still firmly grasped in his, to the bedroom we had never shared. Nerves and tingles of excitement zipped up my spine.

Usually I'd wear a t-shirt to bed, something non restricting and comfortable. But tonight as I did my nightly routine I felt courageous. Sexy almost, as I watched my naked form in the mirror.

I found a racy red negligee in my size in the maternity section when I went shopping for some bigger clothes the other day with Bellamy. I threw it on and marveled at how it felt against my skin.

The satin was top quality, and the lace was trimmed perfectly to outline my breasts. Finn was going to lose his mind, and if he didn't....well I'd just have to make him watch.

When I stepped out of the bathroom Finn's eyes rounded. He stood from where he was seated on the bed. The navy comforter was already drawn down for us to get into.

"Veronica." He said my name like a prayer. Like it was something to worship. "You're not playing fair, Firecracker."

Ronnie

Thirty-Seven

Last night was the first night Finn and I shared our room, it was beautiful and raw. We fell asleep wrapped in each other's arms. His breathing was even and steady, heartbeat pounding in my ear. It was effortless and everything I could have dreamed of.

I wanted to lounge here all day, wrapped in the warmth of him. I traced his brow lightly so I wouldn't wake him, he had wormed his way into my heart and I didn't think I'd ever be rid of him. I knew I didn't want to.

Our baby made it impossible to stay cocooned in bed with Finn. Once I'd get comfortable my little bean would move, or jump on my bladder like a trampoline. He or she was using my body like their very own fun park forcing me out of the bed and to the bathroom.

Washing my hands I stared at my reflection, the smile lines bracketing my lips would have bothered me if I wasn't so fucking happy. So steady in my decision to share my life with

Finn. My eyes looked brighter, and that may or may not be because I'd actually rested while Finn rubbed my back as I drifted off.

He just made me feel safe, *known*.

Xavier had been hounding me for a maternity session since I'd told him and Bellamy that I was pregnant. At thirty-two weeks I didn't feel very beautiful eighty percent of the time, but after last night I felt like I could conquer the world.

I escaped to what I'd dubbed as my closet. Finn painted it a deep emerald and had bought me the vanity dresser I'd been eyeing when we went shopping.

His argument was that the table with one leg shorter than the other was not a suitable table for me to get ready at anymore...because of the bump.

I, of course, rolled my eyes, because it served its purpose just fine.

But, I'd be lying if I said I didn't love the vintage dresser turned makeup artist dream. It had been refinished with my makeup in mind. I didn't know how Finn pulled it off. With the bright lights that surround the mirror and all the storage space.

It was a beautiful piece of furniture, and I loved using it every morning.

Sitting down on the covered stool I decided to do a natural look, sweeping foundation over my face and mascara over my lashes. Finding my dress was the hardest part. I couldn't decide what I wanted to wear.

Xavier didn't give me much in detail about where we'd be taking pictures. Plus, I had zero clue what Finn would be wearing.

I chose a dress that I thought would compliment my growing belly, and match whatever Finn chose to wear.

Taking a deep breath and checking my mirror one more time, I headed out of my room.

Finn looked delicious when I stepped out of my room. He trimmed his beard and tied back his hair in his signature half up-half down mess of waves.

His white Henley fit snug around his mountain muscles, and his dark wash denim jeans looked painted onto his generous thighs. I wouldn't be able to focus on pictures today with him looking like that.

I loved his tattoos and I could see his twin snakes peeking out around his shoulders. The mountains and trees at his wrists, how would I survive this session? He eyed me from head to toe, his lips turned up in the corners just a bit.

"You look..." Finn started, eyes now fixed on mine. "Glowing, Firecracker. You're glowing."

My cheeks got hot and my throat threatened to close. So instead I nodded and twirled for him.

The dress I picked laid just at my knees, form fitting, with sleeves to my elbows. It was a bright blush pink with a plunging neckline to show off my growing breasts.

Throwing on the only pair of converse I owned, thanks to Finn, we made it out the door and into his truck right on time.

Xavier decided to meet us at the location, stating it would be easier for him to set up his equipment early before we got there. Finn drove with one hand on the wheel and the other rubbing on my belly down to my thigh, and back up again.

"Don't be nervous." I said, lacing my fingers in his.

He looked at me briefly and gave me a small smile as he said, "I'm not."

Finn

Thirty-Eight

I lied. I was definitely nervous.

The only time I had professional pictures taken was family photos, and even those only lasted until I'd decided I was old enough not to participate anymore.

Xavier sent me a pin for his location. Which was annoying, but the smile on Ronnie's face when we got there was indescribable.

He had us meet on an abandoned road that had grown over with clover and kudzu. Green surrounded the broken asphalt. Dandelions had grown into the cracks, but the afternoon sun had just started to peek through the foliage.

It was picturesque, even a guy like me could see his vision.

I watched her speak to Xavier as he took a few test shots *to gauge the light* he'd said. Her blonde hair was long and flowing in waves down her back. The setting sun made her look like an angel. Haloed in golden tones her smile was radiant.

She twirled and danced while Xavier threw flower petals and clicked away. The flash of his camera made her come alive. I wasn't exaggerating when I said she was glowing. She was ethereal as she swayed and laughed.

Drops of rain began to lightly fall from the sky.

"Come on baby daddy!" Xavier hollered. "We don't have all day!"

Her blue eyes met mine as I walked toward her. Smiling, I listened to all of her and Xavier's directions, posing and smiling when asked, not smiling when Xavier wanted serious. All for her.

Ronnie was facing Xavier, our hands meeting on her bump, brushing just barely.

I stared at her as Xavier's camera flashed and clicked. She had done her makeup lightly, I could see the freckles that served as my very own constellation. The only way home I knew now.

She needed to know. I couldn't hold it in any longer.

Gently placing my other hand on her chin I tipped her head up to mine. Drops from the sky began falling heavier now, perfect circles of water landed on her upturned face, but she didn't flinch in her unwavering stare.

I scanned the smooth peachy skin of her face, eyes marking everything. Burning her beauty mark right below her right eye into my memory.

"I love you, Firecracker." I told her. "I swear I'll do everything in my power to make you happy for the rest of our lives."

Ronnie

Thirty-Nine

I love you, Firecracker.

I couldn't process the words. Those four words that I had wanted to hear from him, but fear kept me from truly listening.

Finn's tattooed hand threaded our fingers together against my stomach, and the other remained gently cupping my chin. His dark brown irises held nothing but sincerity, dark lashes framed his slightly hooded eyes.

His nose was almost brushing mine, his lips just out of reach. I knew what he wanted, and by God did I want to give it to him. This man who loved me, who wanted to make a life not only for me, but *with* me.

My eyes filled with tears as the rain continued to fall and we stood there, locked in each other. Nothing else mattered, not the click and whir of Xavier's camera, not even the rain.

"Say I'm yours, Firecracker." He breathed against the skin of my neck as tears slid down my face. "Say it, and we can be the family you always wanted. The family you were robbed of."

I couldn't keep denying that I loved him, it wasn't fair to keep holding my feelings in and hurting him. It was starting to erode my heart as well, and seeing him cry made me realize I hadn't been fair to him.

I was suddenly glad I hadn't put more makeup on. As the tears and rain mixed I whispered into his ear. "I love you, Behemoth."

He shifted again, so we were back to where we started. His hand gently cupped my chin, hands firmly grasped under our child in my belly.

Smirking he growled quietly into my ear, "I think I've loved you since the night we fucked in the hallway of my sister's club."

I giggled and pulled back to look at him when his lips crashed down on mine. Moving and commanding, I could feel the love he had for me, for us in this kiss. It was like something out of a fairy tale, something I couldn't even dream of sharing with someone.

But Finn, he made me believe in the impossible.

After Xavier was satisfied with his work, he released us from the limelight.

"Wait, wait!" He cried, "I have something for you!"

He waved his arms around, like Finn and I were already in the truck well on our way home. "Calm down, Xavier." I said with a laugh. "We aren't even that close to the truck."

He produced a shiny silver bag with bright green tissue paper sticking out of the top. "It's something for the baby."

I eyed him and his giddy smile, a little nervous at whatever the gift would be. He didn't want children, and since he was the oldest in the group he probably wouldn't have any now.

Finn held the bag between his hands so mine were free to be used. I pulled the tissue paper out cautiously, or tried to. Xavier sighed and ripped the paper out of the bag. "Hurry up!"

"Pushy!" I said, peering into the bag at the neatly folded fabric at the bottom. I picked it up between my thumb and forefingers. It unfurled as I pulled and the sparkly letters made me snort laugh.

"You rascal!" I laughed, especially at the expression on Finn's face. He was not amused at the little onesie with the words 'My Fairy Godfather is better than your Fairy Godfather' in bright pink writing.

"I had it specially made, just for today." He smirked, snapping photos on his camera.

I caught Finn's smirk out of the corner of my eye, and we all had a laugh as we said goodbye.

***

When we got back, I took the small onesie up to the nursery. Finn joined me not long after, the both of us just soaking in the silence and company of one another. The new rocking chair was plush and sitting in it was like floating on a cloud.

Finn sat on the floor, back against the crib, legs stretched out in front of him.

"I want to take you somewhere you've never been." He said softly.

At first, what he said didn't register. Then, "What do you mean?"

"Well, I've read on a few blogs that people do...like a babymoon, or whatever. It's like a honeymoon, but before the baby comes."

"I can't fly this far along." I didn't want to burst his bubble, he looked so cute sitting there offering to take me somewhere before our baby arrived. "But we could go to the mountains?"

His head snapped back in my direction, "Yeah?"

I nodded and bit my lip. "Yeah."

We talked about a few places as he searched for a place to visit. His sister called and Finn told her about our tentative plan. She squealed and I could hear her when Finn pulled the phone away from his ear. She offered to talk to her friends that just finished building a cabin in Tennessee.

No one had stayed in it yet, so we would have to pack our own linens, dining ware, everything.

"Are you sure they won't mind?" I asked her when Finn put her on speaker.

"Oh, Ronnie! I didn't know y'all were together. How are you feeling?"

I laughed and rubbed my swollen belly. "I'm pretty good, your brother has been an excellent baby daddy."

Finn groaned so loud it's a wonder he didn't vibrate the floor. "I told you not to call me that."

Giselle and I laughed at his expense. We'd met a few times, nothing serious, mainly in passing, but every time Finn spoke to her she asked to speak to me. She was kind, and so funny I felt like we were already friends.

"But really, go, enjoy some time in the peaceful outdoors!" Giselle said before we hung up. "They were planning on renting it out ASAP anyway." Finn said a gentle thank you and goodbye to his sister and ended the call, turning to give me a questioning stare.

"So?" He said.

I shrugged and let him decide. Ultimately it was his sister's friend that was renting out his newly built cabin. "I think you should make this call."

"Let's go." He said, shifting onto his feet he grasped my hands and hauled me out of the chair, and up to our room to pack our bags.

Finn

Forty

Giselle called me early the next morning with what little details her friend could give us. The address, a list of local restaurants to try, and the code to get into the lock box for the keys.

After I'd packed the million things Ronnie swore we needed for our weekend getaway into the truck, I padded upstairs to get her going. It was an early morning, and she had been going to sleep earlier, and sleeping in later.

Pregnancy was hard.

She blinked her eyes slowly awake, the early morning rays were warm, and she stretched like a cat, making obscene noises that had me inwardly groaning.

We wouldn't be going anywhere if she kept doing that.

"Firecracker." I grumbled. She was insatiable recently, and I was more than happy to oblige. In the mountains. Where

I could have her wherever I wanted. "Stop making my dick twitch and get your cute ass in gear."

She cackled, something that made my heart lift in my chest.

"Bossy." She groaned, rolling over to her side and shifting her feet out from the covers. She waddled to the bathroom and I went back down stairs to gather our last minute things. Phone chargers, tooth brushes, deodorant. Things we needed this morning, but didn't want to forget to pack.

"Don't forget your list!" I shouted at the bottom of the stairs.

"Got it!" She yelled back.

I washed the dishes from last night and put her coffee in a thermos for her on the road. She tattered down the stairs, belly swollen and looking absolutely beautiful. Her hair was piled onto her head, she put on one of the new pairs of leggings we'd bought and an oversized sweater.

Flip-flops had been her go-to for a few weeks now, since she couldn't reach much on her body. She slipped them on at the door and kissed me when I handed her the coffee. I took the small bag she'd brought and tucked it under my arm.

"Ready?" I whispered against the shell of her ear.

She nodded enthusiastically and practically ran out the door to the truck.

We stopped at Billy's for her milkshake fix, knowing she wouldn't be able to get one where we were going. Then we were on the road, heading toward our first of many adventures. Her phone rang and she mumbled, "shit, I forgot..."

"Hey, Bell!" She greeted, "I actually meant to call you." She went quiet letting Bellamy talk. "Finn is taking me to the mountains!" She squealed.

"Yeah, yeah. We'll be back Monday." Bellamy must be giving her an earful. "We will, okay, love you, bye!"

"Bellamy says to be careful, and that she will kill you if anything bad happens to me." Ronnie rolled her eyes and laid her head back on the headrest. She dozed on and off the whole trip. We stopped a few times for her to pee, but overall the drive was easy.

When we got close I gently shook her awake. She mumbled and blinked open those deep blue eyes.

"We're almost there, about five minutes." She'd asked me to wake her up when we got close so she could see the house and the mountains.

I had to admit, the view was unlike anything I could have imagined. Green leaves covered the trees in different shades, granite shoulders lined one side of the winding road, and the clouds hung lower the closer we got to the cabin.

It was picturesque, as Ronnie so deemed it when she finally roused from her nap. Her hair was a messy nest on top of her head, and her clothes had shifted from all her movement while she slept.

But with the light filtering through the clouds, she looked more beautiful than I'd ever seen her. Relaxed and content, she looked as if she were finally free. Like she was *living*.

"What?" She asked, covering her mouth with her hand. "Do I have slobber on my chin?"

I chuckled and shook my head, because of course that would be the first thing she thought of.

"No."

"What is it?" She hurried to flip the visor down.

"You're beautiful."

"Okay, so I definitely slobbered then." She found wet wipes from God knew where, and scrubbed at her face until I pulled the truck into the steep driveway of the cabin we would be calling home for the next couple of days.

It was a classic log cabin, stained a warm hickory brown, with three floors. The upper two had balconies, and glass forming the wall. The bottom level was clad with a few windows and a wooden door painted a forest green.

I parked the truck and rounded the hood to help Ronnie out. Any chance I got to touch her, and her growing belly, I took full advantage. I rubbed circles on her stomach and back as she stretched, just waiting for her to get settled before heading into the house.

Ronnie

Forty-One

Finn unlocked the door, the tumble and click of the lock echoed into the forest. When I turned all I could see was the dirt road we had driven up, and trees. So. Many. Trees. I couldn't remember the last time I'd seen this many trees at a time.

I felt like a forest fairy, my hair was longer than it had been in a long time, and I was in a dress that floated around my body like the air itself made it just for me.

"Firecracker," Finn's deep voice boomed through the quiet, "come check the place out with me."

He extended his hand, and I blushed. How long had he stood there staring at me while I played out some fae fantasy in my head?

I took his calloused hand and he guided me inside. The floors were hardwood, the kind that were cut and labored over by hands, not machines. They were stained a rich dark brown with hints of red in the sunlight.

The stairs were covered in light gray carpet, leading to the first floor. It opened up into a brightly lit kitchen and living room. The couch was massive, at least ten or twelve people could lounge on it comfortably, and even though there was no television to be found, it was a trait I found...peaceful. No one came to the mountains to sit and watch TV.

Finn whistled low, "Damn."

"Yeah." I agreed.

The whole place felt a little sterile, since there had been no decor set up yet. It was plain, but I could see the potential. Another staircase led up to where I assumed the bedrooms were, and a loft that would house a pool table, or something of the sort.

Finn opened and closed the deep green cabinets looking for the instructions to turn on the well. Giselle had said her friend left them in a cabinet, but not the specific one.

He pulled a booklet out from one of the bottom cabinets. "Got it!" He said, as if he wasn't sure he would find it.

"I'm gonna go find the breakers, and get the well pumping." He pulled me into his body and kissed my forehead. I smiled into his chest and held his hand until my arms couldn't reach anymore.

"And don't even think about getting the bags!" He hollered from somewhere below. I bit my finger and smiled before venturing up the stairs. Three bedrooms were on this level, all with unmade beds, and no decor.

Not that Finn and I would be up here, the owners suite was behind the kitchen, equipped with its own bathroom and even a full sized closet. I guessed for more storage, if needed.

Carefully heading down the stairs I plopped down in the corner of the couch.

Oh!

Oh, I could get used to this. The couch was snuggly, absolutely perfect as it molded to my sore body, and the view! Holy shit.

The sky was a blue I couldn't even begin to describe. Like freshly spun cotton candy, with perfect white clouds, all overlooking the beautiful green foliage. The trees all seemed to be uniform in some ways.

Like someone had taken giant scissors and cut dips and valleys into the scenery. It was breathtaking, and I understood why this was one of the prime spots of reality everyone wanted a piece of.

I could hear Finn's gruff voice as the door down stairs slammed. "No, Trevor. It isn't fucking working."

I couldn't hear the other, Trevor, end of the conversation. But I could tell it wouldn't be a fun time for whoever he was.

"I followed the exact instructions." Finn hissed, "Well, someone lied to you."

After a few more terse comments Finn hung up and slapped his phone on his leg. "Fuck."

"What's wrong?" I asked, eyeing him over the couch.

He looked up, his face flushed red. "The well pump isn't turning on."

"Okay?"

He laughed, but it didn't feel like a humorous one. "That means we don't have water."

"Oh." I said, eyebrows skyrocketing. "So no showering for the weekend?"

He walked around the sofa and sat down next to me, picking my feet up and sliding under them to massage the swollen appendages.

"It means no toilet, no shower, no bath, no sink. Nothing."

"Are they going to have someone come fix it?" I asked the most logical thing I could.

"It's Saturday, they aren't going to send anyone until Monday." He hung his head and inhaled deeply. "I'm sorry, Ronnie."

"Hey," I cupped his chin, "it's not your fault that the water isn't working."

"We can't stay here for the weekend getaway I'd hoped to give you." His dark eyes were resigned when he looked up at me.

"We can stay for a night." I said, "Surely we can rough it until morning."

He laughed and covered my body with his, careful to avoid our bean. "We can, but you aren't peeing in the woods."

It was my turn to laugh, and when I did I felt our baby move, stirring as if I'd woken the bean from slumber.

Finn ran his hand over my dress, feeling the movement and we sat there for a while, until his belly growled and mine joined him.

"It's wild, you know." He said, hand still circling my tummy. "That our baby is in there, and in a few short weeks we'll meet them, and it will be real."

I placed my hands on his cheeks and forced his eyes to meet mine. "It's already real."

The past two weeks had been incredible, Finn and I went to a few birthing classes, and we put the finishing touches on the nursery. It was beginning to shape up into a real-life fairytale.

Everything was perfect, and Xavier even said the pictures were turning out like some of his best work. It was my first day off in the past two weeks. Ever since we got back from our babymoon I'd been busy going here and there.

Finn asked me on a date, it wasn't uncommon. He liked to call everything a date, it made him feel validated, so I indulged him.

Then he got weird, he pulled out a dress that I'd never bought, asked me to wear it, and told me where we were going was a secret. He had a nice button down on, sleeves rolled to his elbows. Slacks hugged his lean legs and I might have swooned at the sight.

When he finally corralled me into his truck we took off towards my office, I raised a brow at him, increasingly suspicious. He winked, and basically incinerated my underwear.

Fuck, I was so gone for this man.

He pulled the truck into the backlot of my office, mimed zipping his lips and got out. Bellamy met us at the back door, hair curled perfectly in her natural spiral pattern, wearing a dress. A dress, people.

Something was going on, they were acting extra strange.

"Why are you here?" I asked, unsure if I even wanted the answer.

"Surprise!" She shouted, hopping up and down on her toes. She threw her arms around me and giggled in my ear. "It's your baby shower!"

Bellamy had really outdone herself for this baby shower. I shouldn't be surprised, of course she would throw the baby shower of the century. Pastel colors streamed from the ceiling, flowers dotted every surface and Finn was holding my hand while I sat, blown up like a freaking whale with this little baby pushing on my bladder every five minutes.

"Two weeks until my new best friend arrives." Bellamy said, plopping down in the seat on my other side. She gently rubbed my swollen belly, the smile on her face pure joy, and a little teasing.

"New best friend, huh?" I tease back, nudging her soft stomach with my elbow. She tilted her head up to look at me through her lashes. Her hazel eyes widened at the flash of panic that crossed my face. Bellamy had always been able to read me, even when I wished she wouldn't.

"Everything will be fine." She continued running her hand over my stomach, waiting for my little bean to kick, or move. Although, silently I hoped they wouldn't. I'd already been to the bathroom nine billion times in the past hour, and I really didn't want to move.

Their little foot kicked Bellamy's hand and she let out a little squeal of delight, prompting Aaron to head over.

"Can I?" Aaron asked, nodding his head towards my belly. Him and Bellamy went through a lot this past year, and his little gestures like asking for permission to touch my baby bump made me smile.

I nodded, giving him permission. Bellamy guided his hand to where the little being inside of me kicked her hand last.

They did it almost immediately, as if they already knew the two of the most important people in my life.

Bellamy smiled at Aaron, then swung her head to me. "Just so you know, I'm totally taking gender bets at the door." Aaron laughed, and pulled Bellamy up to stand beside him. Placing a gentle kiss on her temple.

Xavier burst through the doors, looking perfectly put together in his signature khakis and blue collared shirt. He'd let his dirty blond hair grow out a bit over these months, something about my belly growing and him growing his hair in solidarity.

Of course Bellamy and I couldn't help but laugh at his antics, especially at his age. He's the oldest out of our little friend group, and he never lets us forget it with all of his 'wisdom'.

His hair was pulled back into a small top knot. The sides of his head, freshly shaved. I knew it because he called yesterday to complain that Bellamy scheduled him to work early, I still couldn't believe I didn't put two and two together. I should have known those two were up to something.

"Where's the baby mama?" I heard him say over the soft music Bellamy had put on Fixin' To I Do's intercom system. Bellamy hooked a thumb over her shoulder in my direction before heading back toward the small kitchen in the office space.

I was suddenly glad it was a floating shower, even if most people had been here since it started. Xavier's blue eyes connected with mine as he pushed his way through the few people blocking his path.

He stopped just shy of my legs, brushing my knees to gently haul me out of the comfy chair and into his arms. "Oh, I can't wait to meet our newest crew member!" He practically yelled in my ear.

Penelope appeared over his shoulder, funny, I hadn't even seen her come in. She had been coming around more recently, joining us on our game nights and dinners. She looked stunning in a pink shirt, and black pants that looked way more comfortable than what Finn insisted I wear today.

"You and me both, Xav," I groaned. "I swear this baby only knows how to dance on my bladder lately. I'll be right back." I wrapped Penelope in a quick hug before waddling towards the small bathroom in the back.

I felt Finn's presence behind me, steady and sure.

I stopped, turning to face him before going into the bathroom to empty what little I had in my bladder. His brown eyes looked sincere and his jaw was tight as if holding back tears. I lifted up on my tippy toes to brush a kiss on his lips when I felt something warm slide down my legs.

"Oh no!" I shouted in his face instead before running into the bathroom and slamming the door. "No, no, no!" I kept chanting.

I could not ruin this dress. It was a gift from Finn, and it was gorgeous.

"Ronnie!" Finn said from the other side of the door. His fists collided with the wood, but I didn't care. Too focused on what I knew was starting to occur.

Wetness continued in a slow trail down my legs, until I sat, then a long powerful rush of water splashed into the toilet. "Oh God!"

"Ronnie! What's wrong!" His voice was panicked, and a small part of me drew strength from that panic. Because I was sure my water just broke.

Finn

Forty-Two

I could hear Ronnie on the other side of the door, desperately saying "no, no, no." But she wasn't answering me. Being this close to her due date I didn't want to take anything lightly.

"Ronnie!" I shouted at the door. "What's wrong?"

I slammed my palm into the door, ready to tear it down if I had to.

The fun loving, pleasure seeking, firecracker I hooked up with all those months ago? She was wild, and daring, but this Ronnie was panicked, and it made my emotions run hot.

"Get Bell!" I heard her scream through the door. Panic felt like a vice being squeezed around my heart.

"Bellamy!" I roared, uncaring of the flinching guests who had significantly grown since Ronnie and I came back here for her to pee. "Come here!"

The curly headed grump poked her head around the corner, looking none too pleased about my tone. I didn't give one single fuck. "Ronnie needs you."

Her narrowed eyes went round, and she bustled around me to the door. It opened enough for her thick body to get through, and slammed into my face once she got through.

"Ronnie!" I heard her all but scream. "You need a hospital!"

A hospital? I knew babies could come early, but now? We still had nine days to go, and we still hadn't agreed on a name. It was hard to do when you didn't even know the sex of your own baby. But Ronnie fought me tooth and nail on it, and ultimately the ultrasound tech did what she wanted anyways.

Fuck.

Was this it?

I didn't wake up this morning expecting to become a dad. I beat on the door again as Aaron turned the corner. He must have seen my face, which I was sure looked pale as fuck.

"What's up?" He asked warily.

"I think Ronnie's in labor." I whispered, just in case I was wrong. Please, let me be wrong. I wasn't ready, fuck, was she ready? My thoughts began like a tilt-a-whirl spinning through my head.

Aaron whistled low, "you think?"

"She was chanting 'no, no, no', so yeah. I think it's time." I ground out, trying and failing to contain my panic. The door flew open and Bellamy's usually tan skin was ashen, her eyes wide.

"What's wrong?" I was a good foot and a half taller than Ronnie's short friend, but I couldn't see Ronnie. Was she on the floor? "Ronnie!" I bellowed.

I could just hear her sniffle, that was all it took. I grabbed Bellamy's shoulders and moved her as gently as possible towards Aaron. Ronnie was on the toilet, tears streaming down her beautiful face. Legs splayed wide, water dotted the dress Bellamy had gotten her just for today.

"Ronnie," I said, kneeling on the bathroom floor in front of her. Wetness dampened my dress slacks. I didn't have time to think about whatever that fluid was though. Unable to ask if she was okay, it was obvious she wasn't.

"Come on," I grabbed her hands. They were fisted in the dress, knuckles turning white. Prying them open so the dress would at least cover her, I pulled her up and walked her out of the cramped space, she doubled over, groaning and panting. She was definitely in labor.

Looks like all those awkward as fuck labor classes paid off.

"Follow us to the hospital after you get everyone out." I gripped Ronnie under her knees and pulled her up into my arms bride style. No way would she make it to the truck and actually be able to get into it.

She didn't protest, and didn't make much noise other than the occasional groan of pain. I managed to get the truck door unlocked and placed her as gently as possible on the seat before buckling her in.

She scream-cursed in pain, clutching herself under her bump. Contractions, I had done enough classes I could probably teach one by now.

"We've got this." I whispered against her forehead. "Me and you."

I leaned back, searching her teary eyes and she nodded.

I ran around the front of the truck and hopped into the driver's seat. Cranked the old bastard, and took off out of the gravel lot behind her work place. It didn't take us long to make it to the little hospital in between the big city and the quarter.

I drove right up to the emergency doors, under the concrete awning of the hospital drive. Tires screeching to a halt, I threw the gear shift into park and flew over to Ronnie's side.

Carrying her into the hospital. She was pale, and her groans of pain had become a little more whimper than groan.

"Labor and delivery, we need a room." I shouted as I made my way toward the nurses station. In this little town, the emergency room only had two or three people sitting in the waiting area.

"Sir, you'll have to wait until I can get a room ready." The nurse said, without looking up. She continued to type on her keyboard, nails clicking on the keys.

Ronnie let out a howl of pain that startled me more than I want to admit. She was writhing in my arms, panting and groaning. God, I hated this. Bringing a baby into the world was no joke. It's why I took all those labor classes without Ronnie knowing. I wanted to be a solid partner in this, for her.

"Lady, point me in the direction of a delivery room." I was ready to rip this woman's head off her shoulders if she didn't get Ronnie taken care of immediately. I paced the waiting area, trying my damndest not to jostle Ronnie.

I wanted to wipe her brow of the little beads of sweat there, but if I moved too much she'd whimper and my heart would jolt.

"Finn!" I turned my head just enough to catch Bellamy bounding towards us. "What's taking so long? I thought she'd be in a room by now!"

She turned her death glare on the nurse at my nod. I was suddenly glad she was here. This was becoming more than I thought I could handle. Ronnie let out another coarse breath, I could hear her gritting her teeth. "Bell." She managed after a beat.

"I'm here." Bellamy said, as softly as I had ever heard her speak. She turned back towards the nurse and I knew shit was about to get worse. "If you don't get her in a room right now, I will find one by my damn self." Her voice was steady, and it even gave me chills.

I couldn't imagine what this nurse felt. Not when her fingernails stilled over the keyboard and her wide eyes found a fuming Bellamy.

"Room 206 is ready. A nurse should be here in a few to get her." She gulped, I watched her throat work, but I didn't feel sorry for her. She didn't seem to care about Ronnie, or the obvious pain and discomfort she was in.

"Don't bother." I said, taking off towards the elevator bank. If I remembered correctly, the labor and delivery unit was on the second floor. I punched the elevator button and we all piled in. "Where's Aaron?"

"He's moving your truck. It was still running when we got here," she said, running the back of her hand over Ronnie's forehead. Offering her comfort in the only way she could at the moment. "He'll be in once he parks it."

I let out a haggard breath. At least he would be here. I knew he wouldn't dare come in the room if Ronnie was ready to push, but just knowing my best friend was here settled the nerves in me.

"It....hurts." Ronnie whimpered. I was too scared to hug her tighter to my chest, so I placed a kiss on her nose.

"I know, we're on our way to the room." I assured her. "We'll get you as comfortable as possible."

The elevator dinged, signaling our arrival. A large woman in black scrubs waited outside the doors with a wheelchair. Once they slid open as far as they could I stepped out with Ronnie and Bellamy.

"I don't want that needle shoved down my back." She said, gripping my shirt in white knuckled fists.

I couldn't hold in the chuckle. That was another thing we had disagreed over. I hated to see Ronnie in pain, and I knew this would be the most painful thing in her life. But she was hellbent on no epidural.

"No needles down your back." Bellamy agreed and greeted the woman hastily. I didn't put Ronnie down. I couldn't bring myself to shift her until we could get her into a bed. We trailed the nurse toward the room we were assigned, our steps hurried.

We entered the large room, lights lit up damn near the whole ceiling. Brown cabinets ran the length of the room to my left, the radiant warmer I made note of on the tour sat to my right, with the bed right in the center.

As gently as possible I laid Ronnie down on the bed, her hands were still fisted into my shirt, unwilling to let go. "Don't leave." She said, her voice broke on the last word as another contraction hit her.

"Never again." I promised.

Ronnie

Forty-Three

Oh *God*! This hurt, and every time I felt like I could get a breath in, another contraction would come along. This baby was going to kill me, this sweet little being I grew in my body would be my downfall.

Of course it would.

My child would be destined to a parentless life, just like I was. I felt tears track down my face, I didn't want to leave him or her without a mother.

I *wouldn't*.

"We need to get you into a gown." The nurse said, jarring me from Finn's face. I nodded and let Finn and the nurse guide the beautiful dress Bell bought off my body. I should have felt something about being naked in a room full of people, but I didn't care.

All I cared about was the thunder of contractions going through my body. The gown was a simple hospital issue, an ugly green that stayed open in the front for nursing. I remember that from the tour Bell and I took a few days ago.

Finn held my hand, unwilling, or unable to move. The nurses bustled about, setting up all the necessary things birthing required. The same nurse from the elevator laid a packaged needle on the bed near the hand Finn wasn't holding.

She was *not* putting that in my body. I flung myself into Finn's side, yelping at the sting of another contraction.

"No." I whimpered. The contractions were getting worse, and I could feel pressure on my pelvis.

"We have to run you a line." She said, her southern drawl grating on my nerves. Usually I found it charming, but nothing right now, especially the woman holding a fucking needle, was charming.

Finn's arms wound around my shoulders, "She doesn't want an epidural."

I was wrong, *his* voice was charming, and soothing, and I wanted to hate him for it. I really did, especially since this was his doing. I knew my brain wasn't being rational. I knew. But him standing there, with his beefy arms around me, made my already frazzled brain react.

I clung to him like a sloth to its young. "Don't let them put that in my back." I cried.

"Shhhh, baby." He said, his lips against my sweaty forehead and his big hand stroking my hair.

"It's not the epidural, it's her IV. We have to get fluids in her." The nurse said so calmly, as if my body wasn't trying to push out a tiny human on its own. She laid her hand on my arm, attempting to pull my death grip off Finn's bicep.

"Please." I begged as another nurse wrapped a monitor around my swollen belly. The monitors around the room started to beep, "What's that?"

The nurse who put it on chuckled a little. "It's a heart monitor for the baby. We just want to make sure your little one is doing okay in there."

I looked up at Finn, his dark chocolate eyes met mine, and it calmed me. Just looking at his pride and hopefulness helped ease my worries. He covered the hand the other nurse was trying to get and pried it off his arm.

My eyes went wide when I realized he was handing it to the nurse. His grip got stronger as I started to panic.

"Hey, Firecracker." He said, his voice low and choked. "You have to do this for the baby, only this once. You're going to be strong, okay? I'll be right here the whole time. I won't let you go."

He had to be uncomfortable, hunched over me with one arm wrapped about my shoulders and the other pinned in his grasp. I nodded and he slowly placed my hand into the nurses.

I didn't want to watch, but I also couldn't not watch as she slid the needle into the topside of my hand. Tears slid from my eyes as pain registered again.

Finn pulled my chin towards him, his lips ghosted over mine before he whispered, "Good girl, mama."

I could have melted, if it weren't for the agonizing pain lancing through my body. His eyes were fierce, but also loving. Fully focused on me, not caring about anything else going on around us.

Bellamy burst into the room with Aaron and my doctor hot on her heels. She came to my other side in a rush to wipe her hand down my face, wiping the tears away. "I found your doctor, she's going to check you and see how far along you are. Okay?"

Doctor Ashton smiled as she washed her hands and covered them in latex. Finn and Aaron hung out by the wall at the head of my bed. "Ronnie, I won't ask how you're doing," she chuckled at her own joke. No one else did, and the room got quiet.

"Let's see how far you've progressed."

While she watched the monitor that recorded my contractions Bellamy held my hand, letting me squeeze when the doctor checked my cervix.

"Ronnie, is there anyone you don't want in this room for birth?" Her eyes were kind, as they always had been but the way they darted towards the back wall where the two men—who were currently pale and quiet stood—I just knew it was time.

Bellamy's grip tightened around my hand, "Do you want us to leave?"

The doctor stood, speaking in low tones to the nurses while I made my decision. "Please stay, Bell." She was the only family I had, and I really couldn't do this without her.

Aaron clapped Finn on the shoulder and planted a kiss on Bellamy's temple before squeezing our clasped hands. "I'll wait outside with Finn's family." He smiled and left, not once looking back.

"Finn." I blew out a steading breath, trying not to cry. I knew I would have to start pushing soon. I could feel the pressure radiating through my hips. "Will you hold my hand?"

His eyes widened, I didn't know if it was shock that I even thought he wouldn't, or if it was something else. "Always."

The doctor and nurses got to work, and with every push it felt like my body was coming apart from the inside. Which I guess it was.

"I can't." I panted as Dr. Ashton asked for one more push, telling me I was doing a great job.

"You can, Firecracker." Finn's deep voice registered by my ear. "You can do anything."

Bell ran a cool cloth over my forehead, wiping away the sweaty mess of my hair. Getting it out of my eyes. Finn's gaze never left mine, encouraging me to push. I nodded at our unspoken agreement and pushed one more time.

A few seconds passed, but it felt like hours before I heard the quiet wail of my baby.

Our baby.

Finn's eyes locked on the naked bundle with a dark head of hair. His eyes instantly watered as the nurses cleaned our baby up and placed him on my chest.

Finn didn't move, he just stared at our son. His eyes wholly focused on him. The gentle slope of his nose, his little ear that was still folded over.

His gentle cry had me in tears, as I sobbed, Bellamy ran her hand over my head. She wasn't a crier, but I knew she was crying too when a tear hit my shoulder. "You did it." Was all she said before she placed a kiss on my cheek and his soft head.

I didn't take my eyes off this precious baby to watch her leave. Presumably to tell the rest of our families the news.

"You have a healthy baby boy, you two," Ashton said, as one of the nurses helped me sit up. My hands instinctively wrapped around our baby's velvet skin so he wouldn't slide. He wiggled in my hold, finding my breast and latching on.

He suckled, and I felt a contraction hit my lower body. Not as strong as before, but noticeable.

Finn laughed, a full belly laugh as my wide eyes met his.

"That's my son." He whispered, and I laughed too. Through the tears I laughed with him, pure joy lit his face, and I had never seen him more handsome than he was right then. I was in love with Finn. Everything felt perfect as I ran a tentative hand over my little bean's head.

As our son ate, he grunted and snorted, it was adorable and Finn watched in rapt fascination.

Dr. Ashton lifted a surgical pair of scissors, "It's time, dad."

Finn looked at me and I nodded, letting him know I was okay, that *we* were okay so he would take his eyes off of us to cut the cord that had nourished our little baby boy. A lone tear leaked down one of his cheeks as he handed the scissors back to Dr. Ashton, and returned to us.

"That's our boy." He said again, as if still in awe that we made something so perfect.

"You did a great job Miss Gibson." The nurse said as she helped the doctor clean me up. "You too, dad." She said to Finn who hadn't stopped staring at us.

The room emptied out as the doctor and nurses finished up doing what they needed to do, telling me they would be back to check on us later.

"He's perfect." I said, gently running my hand over his brow. I had hoped he would get my coloring, but his dark hair looked just like Finn's.

"You're both perfect." Finn said, and our eyes clashed. Mine filled with tears as he pressed his lips to mine. Kissing me breathless. He pulled away, grabbing a chair and pulling it as close as he could to the bed.

Finn

Forty-Four

I had a son.

A son.

I'm a dad, a father.

Holy shit.

Ronnie was a sweaty, fucking beautiful, mess. Her white blond hair was disheveled and her skin still held a sheen of sweat. But she had never looked more beautiful than she did right now.

Holding *our* baby.

The smile that graced her face had me almost on my knees. We would give our son the life she so desperately wanted to.

"He needs a name." Her soft whisper brought me out of that train of thought. She just brought a miracle into the world, and I wanted to soak in the monumental moment.

"You don't have one?"

She shook her head, her eyes glassy once more. "Firecracker," I started, "You don't have to have it all together. We can wait on a name."

Her sea glass eyes, now red rimmed, just stared at me. Her arms wrapped possessively around our baby, her hormones had to be running high after giving birth.

Who knew what it did to her body. I wasn't a patient man, never had been, and I wanted to hold him.

"Finn." She started, a lone tear slipped over her cheek. "He's perfect."

Her lips trembled and I leaned forward. "I know." I ran a hand over the arm that held our baby to her chest. I wanted to hold him so bad I could have wept.

His mouth was still latched to her breast when he squirmed, causing him to lose suction. He didn't cry like I thought he would. Instead he snuggled into her chest and went to sleep. Never blinking once.

"God, Ronnie..." It slipped out of my mouth, "I love you." I couldn't help it. I'd never felt so much since meeting Ronnie. She pushed herself up a little, cradling our child, her eyes lifted to mine.

"And I love you."

I felt my eyes burn hot, before shaking my head as she placed him in my waiting arms. He was so small, much smaller than I thought any living thing could be. But they said he was healthy, and that's all that mattered to me.

I held him as he slept, watched him as his little lips opened and his fat cheeks puffed with every breath of air.

"Atlas." The name came to me while watching him sleep, he looked so peaceful, and if anyone could have brought his mother and I together, it was him. He would be our Atlas, our whole world, because Veronica Gibson was mine, and I was hers.

"Atlas Hart." I tested, watching her face for some sort of reaction. She always overthought everything. But this I was standing firm on. I may be a stubborn bastard, but my son couldn't be known as anything else.

"I love it." She said, almost too quiet.

I kissed her head and made sure she didn't need anything else before the nurse came in again to check on them. Settling Atlas in Ronnie's arms after the nurse cleaned her up and placed something that could only be called a diaper over her bottom, I promised to return once I spoke to everyone waiting.

I knew my mother was probably bursting at the seams to get through this door, but Ronnie wasn't ready, and I wasn't about to push her. Even though we had come leaps and bounds since the start of our relationship Ronnie hadn't yet had the chance to meet my parents.

I didn't expect them all to be here for me and Ronnie, but when I finally entered the room and found almost all of their eyes on me I knew that was a ridiculous thing to think. The hospital waiting room was full of people.

"We have a healthy baby boy." I said to everyone. Aaron grabbed my shoulders and pulled me into a hug. One by one, all of our family and friends hugged me or shook my hand. Congratulations swarmed and all I wanted to do was get back to my woman and our son.

My mom bombarded me with questions as I greeted everyone. Her dark brown hair was up in a top knot on her head, no fly aways to be seen. Her makeup was perfect, always put together.

"Mom, calm down." I heard my sister say from behind me. I was starting to worry her and Benny wouldn't make it in time.

My sister and I looked a lot alike, I guess that happens when you're born only eighteen months apart from each other. Her dark hair and dark eyes met mine before she crushed me in a hug. Benny, her husband, and one of my best friends, slapped me on the back before prying his wife off me.

"How is the baby?" She asked.

"He's perfect." My cheeks hurt from smiling so fucking much, and I was starting to get antsy. "I'm going to go back, I just wanted y'all to know it may be a few hours until you can meet him." I searched the room for my girl's curly headed best friend. "Bellamy, you coming?"

I found her standing by Billy. He was basically a second father to Ronnie and Bellamy. He held my eyes and tilted his head my way in congratulations as Bellamy made her way toward me.

Ronnie

Forty-Five

The nurse took my vitals and gave me some pain medicine, her hands were cold, so when she reached for Atlas I instinctively pulled him back. The nurse just smiled and assured me she wasn't going to take him. She just wanted to get his tag situated, so no one but Finn or I could leave the hospital with him.

I didn't even see the little blue tag in her hands until she wrapped it around his foot and clipped the extra off so it didn't flop around.

"You will have to let us take him to get circumcised, if that's what you and the father have chosen."

I didn't even think about that. The thought of a doctor snipping skin off my child had my monitor going wild. Finn and Bellamy walked in right when the monitor started to chirp.

"Ronnie?" I heard his deep voice start, "What's going on?"

The nurse pulled him aside while Bellamy walked towards the bed. I figured they would move me soon, out of a birthing suite and into a normal room to be monitored overnight. But they hadn't mentioned it yet, and I wasn't going to complain.

"What's wrong?" My best friend asked, her smile faltering when her eyes met mine.

"They have to take him to get circumcised." I almost wailed. I didn't want to think of the pain it would cause him. God, I felt like I was already failing as a mother.

Bellamy stood there, with her arms crossed and her grouchy face on. "Have to?"

"Well, they don't have to. But isn't it the right thing to do?"

She sighed. "The right thing is whatever you think is best for him, Ronnie. Not what the hospital tells you is normally done."

I nodded, my eyes gravitating towards Finn. He had his head down listening to whatever the nurse was telling him intently. He lifted his head and smiled when he caught me staring. The nurse patted his arm and walked out.

"We have a few decisions to make, I hear." His eyes moved over my face before settling on our little bean. "I think we should hear everything Ashton has to say before making a decision."

My mouth dropped open to reply, but honestly, it felt like the right thing to do. To be informed at least. I nodded and Bellamy nudged my arm, silently asking to hold Atlas.

I shifted him into her arms, watching as my best friend melted like she'd never melted before. Atlas made a little squeal of protest before settling into the crook of her arms, and Finn was behind her in a second, hovering over Bell as if she'd hurt him.

"Back up, Behemoth, before I show your son how much of a loser you are."

I laughed, it hurt, and something peculiar flowed out of my unmentionables. I froze in horror, trying to think of all the possible scenarios that could play out.

"Hey, Hey." Finn said, crossing in front of Bellamy to kneel at my side. "What's wrong?" His eyes were unguarded, patient, and open. A lot like how I remember him the morning we woke up from our first night together, wrapped in each other's bodies.

"I, I don't know." Could you bleed out after birth? I think I remember reading that somewhere.

"Tell me what's going on Ronnie, I can't fix it if you don't."

"Something..." I pointed towards the ugly mesh panties the nurse put on me after birth. Whispering only to Finn I said, "I...gushed."

Finn blanched, "You're bleeding?"

"Finn!" I whimpered. Feeling panic and anger rising in one fluid build. "What if I'm dying? Bleeding out while I only just met him!"

"Ronnie. It's okay, remember the doctor said bleeding is normal after birth? She said you'll most likely bleed for a few weeks."

"Weeks?" I screeched. I couldn't take care of a baby and bleed for weeks!

"Do you want me to get the doctor?" Bellamy asked, still looking at baby Atlas.

"No, it's ok. I've got this." Finn replied, "We can deal with some blood, do you want to get up and use the bathroom?"

I looked up as he stood, ready to help me to the bathroom. I was exhausted, I didn't think I could hold myself up, much less remove the mesh underwear diaper thing going on down there. "Bellamy, can you help me?"

Finn's face fell, only for a moment before Bell put Atlas in his arms and helped me hobble towards the bathroom. She helped me get out of the adult diaper and held me up while I relieved my bladder.

It burned and I yelped in surprise. Finn knocked on the door. "Everything alright in there?"

"You just pushed a healthy baby boy out of your body. Things are going to hurt." Bell said, reading my face with precision. I felt my face flush, my hormones were going haywire and I couldn't think straight.

"I'm sorry."

"Why are you apologizing?" She helped me off the toilet and into a new mesh diaper contraption with a giant 'padsicle', as the nurses had called it. Apparently it helped with swelling, but all I cared about was that it felt amazing on my angry, swollen nethers.

"You know, this is quite the fashion statement." She said, making sure the padding was where it needed to be.

I laughed, causing my insides to quiver and my body to hurt. But it felt good, it felt like all the happy endorphins crowded around my heart and squeezed like the best hug in the world.

She helped me to the bed and let me get settled just in time for the pediatrician to come in and explain all the pros and cons of circumcision.

Finn stood there the whole time, rubbing Atlas's back and rocking gently back and forth on his feet. My heart damn near fell out of my chest watching him murmur sweet things to him.

"You know, I think I'll tell everyone to go home for the evening." Bellamy whispered before glancing over her shoulder, patting my hand. "You two enjoy your moment." She said as she walked out the door.

Finn and I were left in silence. Neither one of us spoke, unwilling or afraid to be the one to start. Tears gathered and fell from my eyes as I watched the two of them. Finn, such a large man compared to our tiny baby in his arms, rocking and murmuring to him.

It was enough to split my heart in two.

Finn looked my way quickly, before turning back and looking closer.

"Don't cry." He said, slowly moving in my direction. Placing Atlas in one of his arms so he could wipe away the tears staining my cheeks.

I laughed, an ugly choking noise came out instead. "I'm sorry."

"You don't have to apologize for having feelings, Firecracker."

"No, I'm sorry for not giving us a chance sooner."

His dark eyes widened and a lock of his wavy hair fell into his face, "We're here now, baby."

"I know..." I said.

Finn shook his head, "Don't let that sour this moment."

"I know I hurt you Finn." I started, "And I meant to at the time. I'm sorry for all the lost time we could have had."

"We'll have a lot of time to make up for it." He said leaning down to kiss me. Our lips connected and sparks lit up my insides like Christmas lights.

Ronnie

Forty-Six

The next morning Bellamy and Xavier came by first, he had a cake tin in his hands, and my mouth instantly started to salivate. I hoped it was his orange soda pound cake. My favorite of his baking talents. He always made it for my birthday, and holidays, so I crossed my fingers that it was all for me.

Atlas was bundled up in his bassinet between Finn and I. With a fresh diaper and set of clothes. Xavier cried, like I knew he would, and Bellamy gave me a devilish smirk.

"He is absolutely precious." Xavier proclaimed, as if the room wasn't a metal box that echoed his voice times ten.

Atlas cried, a soft little sound that had all of our attention.

Finn lifted him out of his cocoon and rocked him gently back and forth while Xavier watched in rapt fascination.

"Well, be still my heart. I never thought I'd see the day." He said, hand held over his heart. "Let me have him." It wasn't a question, Xavier made grabby hands after Atlas and we all laughed, except Finn who was currently looking like he wanted to throttle him.

Once Xavier had him settled, he cooed and ahhed while Finn tracked his every move. "Don't think this little monster will get you out of hosting game night." Xavier pursed his lips, "If anything it gives us more of a reason to be there."

Finn groaned but smiled at me.

Bellamy sat on the edge of the mattress, "Finn's family is in the waiting room."

He ran a hand over his face, his beard was unkempt, and his hair was pulled back in a messy knot. "I'll go talk to them."

"Can I meet them?" I asked, sitting up and away from the pillows. I loved Finn and I wanted his family to know just how much he'd grown and become the best man I could have asked for in a partner.

"Only after cake!" Xavier warned.

We laughed and Atlas took the opportunity to have explosive diarrhea. Xavier promptly gave him to Finn with a sour look on his slightly green tinged face. Bell and I lost it, giggles erupted as we watched Finn grimace.

"Hi buddy." Finn began as he changed our baby's nasty diaper, "I'll make you a deal, you never poop again on daddy's watch and I'll pad your inheritance with more money than you could ever need."

"Foul play." I mocked in anger.

"All's fair in love and war, baby." Finn leaned down, brushing my lips with his as he placed Atlas in my arms and left to speak to his parents.

Meeting Finn's family was incredible. He looked just like his mother, and sister. If I didn't already know they weren't, I'd think they were twins. They marveled over Atlas, and asked so many things about me that I couldn't remember everything we talked about.

It was the perfect way to meet them, even non showered and gross. Finn walked them out after an hour. Promising that they could come over whenever they wanted as long as they let us know ahead of time.

He hovered with Atlas in his arms as the nurse helped me into the shower. It was a tad awkward, but I needed to be clean and as fresh as possible. After tonight if we both checked out healthy, Dr. Ass was officially releasing us.

Regina came by with a little care package for mom and baby. Positively smitten with Finn and Atlas, much different from their last meeting. She patted Atlas and returned him to Finn, opting to leave us to grab all of our stuff before Dr. Ashton arrived.

She gave us the all clear and the hospital discharged us shortly after. Soon enough we were in Finn's truck headed back to our house.

Our *home*.

Ronnie

Forty-Seven
(Two Weeks Post Baby)

It was my turn to host game night, and now that we'd moved into the new house I couldn't wait to share this space with my closest friends. Finn already left to go next door, and Bell texted that she was on the way.

Finn went to the grocery store earlier and got everything I asked for. Fruit and a rotisserie chicken, because this mama was too tired to be making one herself. Besides, Xavier probably cooked some amazing sides to go with it, so I wasn't worried.

I'd pumped earlier so that I could enjoy our adult time without having to sacrifice breastfeeding. I was being dramatic, but I wanted to feel like my old self, with Atlas in tow.

He was growing by the day, eyes alert and taking everything in. He was so handsome, with his big blue eyes like mama and dark hair like daddy. His chunky tummy and rollie pollie legs, I could just eat him up with kisses.

Bellamy had been over so much, and the extra pair of hands had been so helpful. I'd showered and napped. Finn had been in and out, working at the gym and helping Aaron with his security gig.

We'd taken a step back from wedding planning, just for a few weeks while we searched for a new client. Our two teams had things well in order, besides, Bell and I never took time off.

It was a needed break.

Xavier and Penelope arrived soon after Bell and I finished putting out all of the fancy serving bowls Finn's mother insisted we would need. As with most things, I was beginning to notice Jolene was right.

She had proven to be an invaluable piece of wisdom and helpfulness that Finn and I needed the first few weeks of Atlas's life. It hadn't felt like the first time we met was at the hospital when she agreed to stay with us for a few weeks while we got settled into a new routine.

She felt like what I imagined my mother would be in those moments. With her nurturing hands and soothing demeanor, Jolene felt like a security, much like her son. I still had trouble wrapping my brain around the fact that I could have such feelings about the mother of the love of my life. Without feeling the fear and insecurity of losing them.

"Where is my baby boy?" Xavier cooed, pulling me from my thoughts. He made his way over to Bellamy, who was burping Atlas. He dumped the things in his arms on the bar unceremoniously.

"You hold him, you change him." I lifted my shoulders, "New players, new game rules."

He scoffed, but took Atlas from Bell and rocked him back and forth in his arms. Penelope carried in more items and I helped her put them where they needed to go.

"And where is the lovely, Jolene?" Xavier asked Atlas in his best baby talk.

"She left late yesterday," I made Finn call her this morning to make sure she made it home safe, "She's probably hours into a nap right about now." I teased.

"She's a saint, that woman." Bellamy said, taking the words right out of my brain.

We plated food and ate, all while everyone got their fix of Atlas. He made a few sounds and wildly moved his little arms. We blew him kisses and he smiled a gummy smile.

Finn, Aaron, and Benny all came in for food. However, another figure stalked through the doorway and we all looked to Xavier, I didn't know Landon would be with them. The last time Finn talked about him he was headed back to North Carolina, after Xavier fired him from New Leaf.

Finn kissed my head and rubbed Atlas's belly.

"I didn't know you were still in town, Landon." Bellamy said, voice like ice.

Ouch.

He smiled, "Just came back, had to tie up a few loose ends."

Looks were exchanged as I stood with Atlas and laid him in his portable bassinet. He sucked on his paci and went to sleep. He'd be up in a few hours, ready to eat again.

Finn rounded the stairs after me and slid his arms around my hips, I wasn't in perfect shape. I had a lot of pooch now that all the skin I'd stretched with Atlas was no longer stretched. But he used every excuse he could to touch me and shower me with compliments.

"You didn't tell me Landon was coming." I admonished.

"Thought it might be a nice surprise." Finn whispered in my ear mischievously.

I turned and lifted my arms to link my hands behind his neck, the instant our lips touched I felt fireworks. Great ground shuddering fireworks, bright colorful strokes of light filtered behind my eyelids.

"I love you." We said it at the same time, both smiling into each other's kisses.

We returned to the table, where Xavier was giving Landon a death glare. Bellamy and Aaron were holding hands under the table, and Penelope was rolling her eyes at Xavier's rude behavior.

Finn loaded up his plate and sat next to me at the table, when he sat, his gaze caught mine, and I smirked. He was the sexiest man I'd ever met, hands down. Seeing him being such a good father to Atlas had me ready for Dr. Steele to release me already so I could jump his bones.

"Alright you two." Xavier muttered.

"Sorry, what was that sour puss?" Penelope asked.

"Ugh!" Xavier groaned, "Stop looking at my best friend like you want to eat *her* for dinner instead."

Finn winked at him and said, "It's been a long six weeks, man."

Xavier looked at me incredulously, like I was scandalizing the whole lot of us. I'd show him. I smirked, shrugged my shoulders and said, "Can't help I have a bomb ass pussy."

Rowdy laughter and cat calls sounded over the table as we all finally dug into our meals. My heart felt like it could burst. My home, filled with the people I loved, laughter flowed, voices floated, it was perfect.

Bellamy and Aaron were happily chatting with Penelope between bites, Benny and Landon were talking about whatever sports team would come out of top this year, and Xavier was staring daggers at Landon, who, to his credit, ignored the sharp eyes.

And then there were my two guys. Finn turned his head to look at our son, always hawk eyed and ready for anything. I leaned over placing my chin on Finn's shoulder, "We did it."

He smiled, and turned to kiss my forehead, "We did, Firecracker."

Finn

After
(Two Years Later)

If you knew me five years ago, you never would have caught me dead at a child's birthday party. Or wearing a fucking bunny costume at said birthday party. But what my baby wanted, my baby got.

Ronnie, that is.

She had this grand second birthday planned out, which involved a visit from an overly grown bunny. Also known as me. I'd put the costume on in the garage while Aaron held my beer and laughed at my expense.

"You just wait until y'all have one, fucker." I told him. It wouldn't be long. Not with their wedding in a few short weeks. I'd noticed Bellamy's eyes linger longer on Atlas, eyes looking far away, as if she could see her own future.

"The costume fits you so well!" He said, doubling over once I had put the head on. I looked like an absolute fucking nightmare. What rabbit was over six foot tall and smiling all the time? Not a sane one. This was creepy as hell, I didn't know what Ronnie was thinking.

But what made my Firecracker happy, made me happy. Even the cheesy invitations, "Some Bunny is Turning Two!" were extravagant. Her and Bellamy had decorated the backyard all day yesterday in preparation for today.

"And here he comes! Peter Cottontail hopping through the grass!" Ronnie sang to our baby boy. Atlas was getting big, his curly brown hair had lightened up since birth, and I loved it. It was as if his shade of brown was the perfect mix of mine and his mothers.

His eyes were a deep green that neither of us could figure out, his little grin and bubbling laughter made this whole bunny costume worth it. My boy loved bunnies.

Chunky arms flew through the air as he cackled. I hopped and wiggled my ass over to where Ronnie stood with Atlas. His little hands opened and reached for me. Gathering him in my arms he pulled on the dropping ears of the costume, trying to put them in his slobbery mouth.

He was cutting more teeth, which had been hell for us. But we took it all in stride, who needed a full, uninterrupted eight hour sleep anyways. Honestly my Firecracker and I couldn't have been more perfect for each other. Soulmates, or whatever Ronnie liked to call it.

After a few parades around the yard, Ronnie hollered that Peter Cottontail needed to go home. Thank fuck, this thing was hot, and I was sweating under the hot furry brown cloth.

Aaron took Atlas who had become his new best friend, much to Bellamy's dismay. She placed her hands on her hips and said, "Boy! That's my man!"

I could hear Atlas cackling as Aaron and Bellamy tickled and loved on him. My dad met me in the garage to help me get out of this costume.

When I had finally shed all the layers dad clapped me on the back and said, "You done good, son."

"Thank you, dad." I told him.

My parents had been instrumental in helping Ronnie and I navigate parenthood. When we had a question, either mom or dad was there with an answer. They knew all the right things to say, and had the best advice for damn near everything.

We walked back to the backyard where Xavier was chasing Atlas around in the grass. He had his favorite stuffed bunny in the crook of one arm, legs teetering as he ran and screeched when Xavier pretended he couldn't catch him.

It had been the best two years of my life.

Easily.

I had never been happier than I was when Ronnie came home from work, or when Atlas tried to string words together. Watching him grow had been the best honor I'd ever received, and as for Ronnie and I? We were in sync, it was rare that we would ever fight, and when we did I always made it up to her in the ways it counted.

Ronnie slipped her arms around my middle, resting her head on my stomach. "We did that."

"We did." I agreed, running my hand down her hair. She had gotten it cut not long ago, during her monthly mommy time. It looked like it did when we met, after she cut so much of it off.

She leaned back to look up at me, smiling that beautiful smile before kissing the underside of my jaw and turning away. She scooped Atlas up and planted kisses all over his face.

"Okay!" She shouted, gathering everyone's attention. "Time for cake!"

My mother carried it out of the house, two little candles were lit in the center with bunnies decorating the top. She started singing 'Happy Birthday' and we all joined in as Atlas looked around.

Ronnie and I helped him blow out the candles and Atlas picked now to shout his new favorite word, "Shit!"

We cut our eyes at Aaron who was trying to hold in a laugh. "I'm sorry!" He finally got out after his bout of laughter. "I didn't know he was in the room!"

Mine and Ronnie's phone pinged with a notification. It was one of our front cameras letting us know someone had pulled in our driveway. Since everyone was already here I frowned and looked at Ronnie, who looked back at me equally baffled. I set my drink down and ruffled Atlas's hair before heading around the house only to spot Landon running up to the front door and pounding on it.

"Landon!" I said, "It's good to see you, man."

Landon rushed over to me, looking a little worse for wear.

His eyes looked red, as if he'd been crying and I wanted to ask what was wrong, but before I could, he spoke.

"I'm sorry to show up like this. I didn't plan on it but I need to speak to Xavier." He rushed out. "Right now."

Ronnie

After

Xavier didn't come back to the party after Landon's surprise arrival. Bell and I had given him hugs and promised to call and check on him tomorrow. I would have offered Penelope the guest room in my house, but Finn's parents were staying another night. So she would be crashing on Bell's couch tonight.

We cleaned everything up, it made me a little sad. My baby only turned two once, and it just never felt like enough. Finn and Aaron were sucking the helium out of the bunny balloons and saying stupid shit to each other.

"Men." Bell huffed.

I laughed, "Men? More like boys."

"Hey! Who you callin' boys?" Finn shouted in the high pitch whine of helium. He and Aaron doubled over in laughter, and we couldn't help but to join them.

Jolene and Sutton had done all the dishes by the time Bell and I got everything else cleared and walked into the house.

Atlas was shouting, "mama!" every time Penelope asked him to say "P", and she was cracking up.

"Atlas." I sign-songed, "Do you want me or daddy to read you a book tonight?"

It was way past his bedtime, and he rubbed his little eyes as he pulled his blankie behind him over to me. "Paw!"

Sutton lifted his fist in victory. "Atta boy!"

He scooped him into his arms and carried him up the stairs to get him ready for bed. I was exhausted, and thankful for the extra hands tonight.

"We'll have him ready for bed in no time." Jolene patted my shoulder as she walked by. "Enjoy some alone time with your friends."

I heard the tub start up, and the patter of feet as Atlas ran down the hall, when he passed the top of the stairs I saw his naked little butt turn and run away from Jolene, right back into Sutton's grip if the squeals of delight were any indication.

My heart swelled at the pure glee in my son's voice as he made memories with his grandparents. Memories that I hoped lasted a lifetime.

I saw Finn's tattooed hands before he placed them on my shoulders. "I'm sending everyone home, Firecracker." The fresh ink on his left ring finger flashed in my peripheral as he gripped my neck and bent it back so I could see him. "You're all mine tonight, baby."

His lips ghosted over mine, a sinful smile pulling them away.

"Bell, Pen, you gotta go." I said playfully, hooking my thumb toward the door.

They laughed and we hugged as we said goodbye. Then it was just us, standing in our home with our child splashing water everywhere, and Finn's parents pretending to be upset about it.

Finn chuckled and pulled my body into his by my hips, I looped my arms around his neck and we stood like that, enjoying the sounds of our life. Enjoying the little moment of peace before we kissed our little man and let him sleep.

"Come with me?" He whispered in my ear.

"Anywhere." I answered.

We walked hand in hand to the bathroom where Atlas had indeed gotten water everywhere and was standing in his little red robe while Jolene combed his curly hair. Sutton handed him his toothbrush and helped him brush what teeth he had.

"Teef!" Atlas said when he finally noticed us standing in the doorway.

"Teeth, buddy." Finn agreed. "Goodnight book?'

"Paw!" He pointed at Sutton.

I bent down and I opened my arms, Atlas threw his toothbrush and bolted into them. I wrapped him up tight and kissed his cheeks, and nose. He kissed my mouth, openly of course, and scrambled out of my arms toward Finn to do the same.

Running the back of my hand over my lips to get rid of the strawberry flavored slobber, I turned. Watching Finn love on Atlas was one of my favorite things to do. This big, tattooed, muscled man held our little boy with so much love I almost teared up.

Jolene wrestled him away from Finn and said, "Time for your bedtime story, wild one."

Sutton cleaned up the bathroom while Jolene put Atlas in his pajamas, and Finn and I headed toward our bedroom.

When the door closed behind Finn it felt like a whole new world. Finn had the foresight to have our room soundproofed during the time I'd debated moving in, and it was the best thing he could have done.

We couldn't keep our hands off each other, no matter how tired we were. Our magnetism never wavered, thank God.

Finn stood with his back against the door, "Strip for me, Firecracker."

Panties, wet.

Fuck I loved his voice, and when he gave me commands I felt like I could combust on the spot at whenever he asked. I knew he'd want to play, especially after the bunny costume. And oh what a good boy he had been too.

I licked my lips, making sure to drag my teeth over my bottom lip as I slowly pulled off my shirt. His eyes burned as

I shimmed out of my pants. Standing in front of him, waiting for him to tell me what he wanted, in only a black lacy bra and thong, felt powerful and I fucking lived for it.

"Come here and get on your knees for me, baby." He crooned, "Goddamn, do you know how fucking divine you are?"

I nodded my head, because I wanted to be the one in control tonight. Slinking my way over to him, I made sure to sway my hips and run my hands over his shoulders, chest, abdominals, and thighs on my way to kneel at his feet.

"Good girl." He praised, running one hand down my cheek and using the other to undo his belt. I couldn't wait to taste him, to bring him to *his* knees. I freed his cock from his boxers, the sight never got old, and licked the drop of precum from his tip.

His intake of breath sent shivers down my spine, and I licked him from base to tip, making sure to fatten my tongue so he could look down and enjoy the view.

"*Fuck*," he said, leaning his head back against the door.

Taking him into my mouth I began working in light, teasing strokes. Sucking and licking, using my hand to get to what my mouth couldn't. Spit pooled in my mouth and ran over my lips as I continued lavishing his cock.

"Goddamn it." He rumbled and freed himself from my mouth. "That dirty mouth of yours is going to ruin all my fun."

Easily he hefted me over his shoulder and I cackled, enjoying the view and knowing exactly where he was taking me.

He flipped on the shower and set me on the cold counter to watch him strip. His body was stunning, everything from the toned muscles, to the dark sprinkling of hair on his chest that led a path down his stomach.

He shucked his boxers and picked me back up. I wrapped my legs around his hips and gripped his shoulders, as he walked us into the steaming water. Our lips met in frenzied movements.

Nipping at my bottom lip he moaned, water cascaded over his face, long eyelashes dripping. He was the sexiest man alive, and he was all mine. He set me on my feet, sliding me down his body so his cock rubbed my pussy.

"I love you," I groaned.

"I know." He smiled a cocky grin, "Now turn around so I can fuck that drenched pussy."

I did as he commanded, bending over and grabbing my ankles. His palms slid over my slicked skin, squeezing and kneading my ass. He pumped two fingers inside of me and I whimpered incoherent words for more.

Swiftly he replaced his fingers with the tip of his cock, "You ready, baby?"

"Fuck, yes." I hissed, more than ready for him to rock my world.

He slid hard into my cunt, making me cry out at the delicious heat of us together. He moved leisurely in circles grinding against my ass.

"More." I panted.

He obliged, pounding into me, hitting new angles and building my release higher and higher until I couldn't fucking hold it. I wailed with bliss as my orgasm barreled through me. The sound of our skin slapping together and the way he wrapped his hand around my hip while snaking the other around to my clit to strum it with perfect strokes had me spiraling into a second one. Cum rushed out of my pussy, coating his cock and legs with my pleasure.

"*Goddamn.*" His voice rumbled, and I felt it in my toes. "Fuck, Ronnie."

I could only whimper and moan in response, as he lifted me up, spun me around, and backed me up against the cool glass.

"You." He kissed my lips. "Are." He kissed my neck. "Mine." He bit the sensitive flesh where my neck met my shoulder, and lifted my leg around his hip, plunging back into me. My eyes rolled back at the absolute pleasure he had already wrung from my body, enjoying the aftershocks that accompanied his movements.

He peppered my breasts with nips and kisses as he moved inside of me, seeking his own release. His hand wrapped around my throat and he brought our lips together as he spilt himself inside of me, groaning my name like a prayer.

We stood there for a moment, trading tender kisses, hands roving each other's bodies as we came down from the high.

"I fucking love you, Ronnie. You're the best thing that's ever happened to me." He said, lathering up suds on a cloth to wash us off. He ran the fluffy cloth over my sensitive body, making sure to reach every nook and cranny. When he was satisfied he twirled me around to massage shampoo into my hair.

I rinsed it out as he cleaned himself, and stood on the built in bench to return the favor of massaging his scalp. When he was finished he wrapped me in a towel and ran curl cream through my hair and his.

We traded kisses instead of words as we dried off and slid between the cool sheets of our bed. When we both settled, my cheek on his chest, his arm slung over my side, our legs tangled together he whispered, "Say it, Firecracker."

I smiled and said against his skin, "You're mine."

Acknowledgements

If you've ever heard the phrase "it takes a village", it can apply to anything. And my, what a village I have.

Ronnie and Finn's story was hard for me to write. I missed my first two deadlines because I just wasn't in the right headspace to write these characters in the way they deserved. I felt like a failure, and contemplated not writing them at all.

Imposter syndrome is a real bitch.

Enter my village....

Kenny, you consistently keep my head above water. Your silent encouragement is cherished, and I am forever grateful for a partner like you.

Grandma Kitty, I love you. Plain and simple. My dreams wouldn't be as big and bold as they are if it weren't for you and Grandpa. Thank you for loving me without boundaries, for showing me what it means to be a genuine person, and for never giving up on me. You are one of the strongest women I know, and I am honored to call you Grandma.

Mama, thank you for being as excited as I was when I got proof copies of my first book. Thank you for loving me for who I am, even when I was, and still can be, an asshole. (Also, please ignore my use of cuss words.) Todd, I have no words for the amount of joy your encouragement of my writing brings me, other than thank you. I love you both, so much.

Dad, thank you for showing me your love for literature. If it weren't for you, I probably would have never started reading, much less attempted to become an author. Love you bunches.

Tina, *my word*. My soundboard, you always listen to my many ideas and encourage me to follow wherever they lead. If it weren't for you, Ronnie wouldn't exist.

Trinity, my trusted editor and friend. You are invaluable, Firecracker wouldn't be possible without your guidance and tender hand. I love your brain, and the way you push me to be a better author.

Jessica, the ultimate hype woman. This dream wouldn't be possible without your belief in me. You have so much faith in me to write good stories, and I hope I live up to your expectations.

Karley, my talented friend. I wouldn't even know where to start without your help. Your cover design and formatting is always perfect, like you've crawled inside my brain and picked it right out.

Ashley, I love that even though romance isn't your favorite genre, you are always down to read whatever I write. Your critique helps push me to be a better author, and I don't think I'd feel half as confident putting Firecracker out there without your help.

To my ARC readers and Street Team, thank you so much for reading my words! I hope they help you find happiness!

Readers, thank you for taking a chance on my books. None of this, from my debut to anything I publish in the future, would be possible without you. I am truly grateful for each and every one of you, and I hope you come to love these characters as much as I do.

Here's to many more!

About the Author

Taylor Wilson-West is a firm believer that the magic of words on a page can transport readers to new places, and finds comfort in making new, albeit fictional, friends. Currently residing in a small town in North Carolina with her husband and two perfect kiddos, she lives off Cheerwine, potatoes, and ranch dressing. When she's not reading or writing, she can be found shopping at bookstores, adding to her never ending bookshelves. Taylor finds it necessary to have a bookish candle that fits every genre and book character that she has ever fallen in love with. Her favorite moment in any consumable media is when confident, fat main characters get their happily ever after.

If you've made it this far, please leave a review! Reviews are an author's best friend, and readers obviously! :P

taylorwilsonwest.com

Find her @25thavenuewest on all social media!

Also By

Taylor Wilson-West

Say I Do, Sunshine

Milton Keynes UK
Ingram Content Group UK Ltd.
UKHW040801291223
435170UK00001B/35

9 798988 396925